Sandra Marton is the author of over 30 books for Harlequin Presents. Here's what the reviewers said about her book, A PROPER WIFE:

"The Brilliant storyteller Sandra Marton...pens an impassioned tale brimming with vividly real characters, thrilling scenes and simply crackling chemistry... Another sure keeper for your bookshelf."
—*Romantic Times*
(Awarded RT's Gold Medal.)

"Ms. Marton has written a super entertaining story full of conflict, humor, romance and love. An excellent read."
—*Rendezvous Magazine*

SANDRA MARTON is the author of more than thirty romance novels. Readers around the world love her strong, passionate heroes and determined, spirited heroines. When she's not writing, Sandra likes to hike, read, explore out-of-the-way restaurants and travel to faraway places. The mother of two grown sons, Sandra lives with her husband in a sun-filled house in a quiet corner of Connecticut where she alternates between extravagant bouts of gourmet cooking and take-out pizza. You can write to her (SASE) at P.O. Box 295, Storrs, Connecticut 06268.

Books by Sandra Marton

SANDRA MARTON

The Second Mrs Adams

Harlequin Books

TORONTO • NEW YORK • LONDON
AMSTERDAM • PARÍS • SYDNEY • HAMBURG
STOCKHOLM • ATHENS • TOKYO • MILAN
MADRID • WARSAW • BUDAPEST • AUCKLAND

ISBN 0-373-11899-6

THE SECOND MRS ADAMS

First North American Publication 1997.

Copyright © 1996 by Sandra Myles.

This edition published by arrangement with Harlequin Books S.A.

Printed in U.S.A.

CHAPTER ONE

THE siren was loud.

Painfully, agonizingly loud.

The sound was a live thing, burrowing deep into her skull, tunneling into the marrow of her bones.

Make it stop, she thought, oh please, make it stop.

But even when it did, the silence didn't take the pain away.

"My head," she whispered. "My head."

No one was listening. Or perhaps no one could hear her. Was she really saying anything or was she only thinking the words?

People were crowded around, faces looking down at her, some white with concern, others sweaty with curiosity. Hands were moving over her now, very gently, and then they were lifting her; oh, God, it hurt!

"Easy," somebody said, and then she was inside a...a what? A truck? No. It was an ambulance. And now the doors closed and the ambulance began to move and the sound, that awful sound, began again and they were flying through the streets.

Terror constricted her throat.

What's happened to me? she thought desperately.

She tried to gasp out the words but she couldn't form them. She was trapped in silence and in pain as they raced through the city.

Had there been an accident? A picture formed in her mind of wet, glistening pavement, a curb, a taxi hurtling toward her. She heard again the bleat of a horn and the squeal of tires seeking a purchase that was not to be found...

No. No! she thought, and then she screamed her denial but

the scream rose to mingle with the wail of the siren as she tumbled down into velvet darkness.

She lay on her back and drifted in the blue waters of a dream. There was a bright yellow light overhead.

Was it the sun?

There were voices… Disembodied voices, floating on the air. Sentence fragments that made no sense, falling around her with the coldness of snow.

"…five more CC's…"

"…blood pressure not stabilized yet…"

"…wait for a CAT scan before…"

The voices droned on. It wasn't anything to do with her, she decided drowsily, and fell back into the darkness.

The next time she awoke, the voices were still talking.

"…no prognosis, at this stage…"

"…touch and go for a while, but…"

They *were* talking about her. But why? What was wrong with her? She wanted to ask, she wanted to tell them to stop discussing her as if she weren't there because she *was* there, it was just that she couldn't get her eyes to open because the lids were so heavy.

She groaned and a hand closed over hers, the fingers gripping hers reassuringly.

"Joanna?"

Who?

"Joanna, can you hear me?"

Joanna? Was that who she was? Was that her name?

"…head injuries are often unpredictable…"

The hand tightened on hers. "Dammit, stop talking about her as if she weren't here!"

The voice was as masculine as the touch, blunt with anger and command. Blessedly, the buzz of words ceased. Joanna tried to move her fingers, to press them against the ones that clasped hers and let the man know she was grateful for what he'd done, but she couldn't. Though her mind willed it, her hand wouldn't respond. It felt like the rest of her, as lifeless as a lump of lead. She could only lie there unmoving, her fingers caught within those of the stranger's.

"It's all right, Joanna," he murmured. "I'm here."

His voice soothed her but his words sent fear coursing through her blood. Who? she thought wildly, who was here?

Without warning, the blackness opened beneath her and sucked her down.

When she awoke next, it was to silence.

She knew at once that she was alone. There were no voices, no hand holding hers. And though she felt as if she were floating, her mind felt clear.

Would she be able to open her eyes this time? The possibility that she couldn't terrified her. Was she paralyzed? No. Her toes moved, and her fingers. Her hands, her legs...

All right, then.

Joanna took a breath, held it, then slowly let it out. Then she raised eyelids that felt as if they had been coated with cement.

The sudden rush of light was almost blinding. She blinked against it and looked around her.

She was in a hospital room. There was no mistaking it for anything else. The high ceiling and the bottle suspended beside the bed, dripping something pale and colorless into her vein, confirmed it.

The room was not unpleasant. It was large, drenched in bright sunlight and filled with baskets of fruit and vases of flowers.

Was all that for her? It had to be; hers was the only bed in the room.

What had happened to her? She had seen no cast on her legs or her arms; nothing ached in her body or her limbs. Except for the slender plastic tubing snaking into her arm, she might have awakened from a nap.

Was there a bell to ring? She lifted her head from the pillow. Surely there was a way to call some...

"Ahh!"

Pain lanced through her skull with the keenness of a knife. She fell back and shut her eyes against it.

"Mrs. Adams?"

Joanna's breath hissed from between her teeth.

"Mrs. Adams, do you hear me? Open your eyes, please, Mrs. Adams, and look at me."

It hurt, God, it hurt, but she managed to look up into a stern female face that was instantly softened by a smile.

"That's the way, Mrs. Adams. Good girl. How do you feel?"

Joanna opened her mouth but nothing came out. The nurse nodded sympathetically.

"Wait a moment. Let me moisten your lips with some ice chips. There, how's that?"

"My head hurts," Joanna said in a cracked whisper.

The nurse's smile broadened, as if something wonderful had happened.

"Of course it does, dear. I'm sure the doctor will give you something for it as soon as he's seen you. I'll just go and get him..."

Joanna's hand shot out. She caught the edge of the woman's crisp white sleeve.

"Please," she said, "what happened to me?"

"Doctor Corbett will explain everything, Mrs. Adams."

"Was I in an accident? I don't remember. A car. A taxi..."

"Hush now, dear." The woman extricated herself gently from Joanna's grasp and made her way toward the door. "Just lie back and relax, Mrs. Adams. I'll only be a moment."

"Wait!"

The single word stopped the nurse with its urgency. She paused in the doorway and swung around.

"What is it, Mrs. Adams?"

Joanna stared at the round, kindly face. She felt the seconds flying away from her with every pounding beat of her heart.

"You keep calling me...you keep saying, 'Mrs. Adams...'"

She saw the sudden twist in the nurse's mouth, the dawning of sympathetic realization in the woman's eyes.

"Can you tell me," Joanna said in a broken whisper, "can you tell me who... What I mean is, could you tell me, please, who I am?"

The doctor came. Two doctors, actually, one a pleasant young man with a gentle touch and another, an older man with a patrician air and a way of looking at her as if she weren't really there while he poked and prodded but that was OK because Joanna felt as if she wasn't really there, surely not here in this bed, in this room, without any idea in the world of who she was.

"Mrs. Adams" they all called her, and like some well-trained dog, she learned within moments to answer to the name, to extend her arm and let them take out the tubing, to say "Yes?" when one of them addressed her by the name, but who was Mrs. Adams?

Joanna only knew that she was here, in this room, and that to all intents and purposes, her life had begun an hour before.

She asked questions, the kind she'd never heard anywhere but in a bad movie and even when she thought that, it amazed her that she'd know there was such a thing as a bad movie.

But the doctor, the young one, said that was what amnesia was like, that you remembered some things and not others, that it wasn't as if your brain had been wiped clean of everything, and Joanna thought thank goodness for that or she would lie here like a giant turnip. She said as much to the young doctor and he laughed and she laughed, even though it hurt her head when she did, and then, without any warning, she wasn't laughing at all, she was sobbing as if her heart were going to break, and a needle slid into her arm and she fell into oblivion.

It was nighttime when she woke next.

The room was dark, except for the light seeping in from the hushed silence of the corridor just outside the partly open door. The blackness beyond the windowpane was broken by the glow of lights from what surely had to be a city.

Joanna stirred restlessly. "Nurse?" she whispered.

"Joanna."

She knew the voice. It was the same masculine one that she'd heard an eternity ago when she'd surfaced from unconsciousness.

"Yes," she said.

She heard the soft creak of leather and a shape rose from the chair beside her bed. Slowly, carefully, she turned her head on the pillow.

His figure was shrouded in shadow, his face indistinct. She could see only that he was big and broad of shoulder, that he seemed powerful, almost mystical in the darkness.

"Joanna," he said again, his voice gruff as she'd remembered it yet tinged now with a husky softness. His hand closed over hers and this time she had no difficulty flexing her fingers and threading them through his, clasping his hand and holding on as if to a lifeline. "Welcome back," he said, and she could hear the smile and the relief in the words.

Joanna swallowed hard. There was so much she wanted to ask, but it seemed so stupid to say, "who am I?" or "who are you?" or "where am I?" or "how did I get here?"

"You probably have a lot of questions," he said, and she almost sobbed with relief.

"Yes," she murmured.

He nodded. "Ask them, then—or shall I get the nurse first? Do you need anything? Want anything? Water, or some cracked ice, or perhaps you need to go to the bathroom?"

"Answers," Joanna said urgently, her hand tightening on his, "I need answers."

"Of course. Shall I turn up the light?"

"No," she said quickly. If he turned up the light, this would all become real. And it wasn't real. It couldn't be. "No, it's fine this way, thank you."

"Very well, then." The bed sighed as he sat down beside her. His hip brushed against hers, and she could feel the heat of him, the strength and the power. "Ask away, and I'll do my best to answer."

Joanna licked her lips. "What—what happened? I mean, how did I get here? Was there an accident?"

He sighed. "Yes."

"I seem to remember... I don't know. It was raining, I think."

"Yes," he said again. His hand tightened on hers. "It was."

"I stepped off the curb. The light was with me, I'd checked because...because..." She frowned. There was a reason, she knew there was, and it had something to do with him, but how could it when she didn't...when she had no idea who he...

Joanna whimpered, and the man bent down and clasped her shoulders.

"It's all right," he said, "it's all right, Joanna."

It wasn't, though. The touch of his hands on her was gentle but she could feel the tightly leashed rage in him, smell its hot, masculine scent on the carefully filtered hospital air.

"The taxi..."

"Yes."

"It—it came flying through the intersection..."

"Hush."

"I saw it, but by the time I did it was too late..."

Her voice quavered, then broke. The man cursed softly and his hands slid beneath her back and he lifted her toward him, cradling her against his chest.

Pain bloomed like an evil, white-hot flower behind her eyes. A cry rose in her throat and burst from her lips. Instantly, he lay her back against the pillows.

"Hell," he said. "I'm sorry, Joanna. I shouldn't have moved you."

Strangely, the instant of pain had been a small price to pay for the comfort she'd felt in his arms. His strength had seemed to flow into her body; his heartbeat had seemed to give determination to hers.

She wanted to tell him that, but how did you say such things to a stranger?

"Joanna? Are you all right?"

She nodded. "I'm fine. I just—I have so many questions…"

He brushed the back of his hand along her cheek in a wordless gesture.

"I need to know." She took a breath. "Tell me the rest, please. The taxi hit me, didn't it?"

"Yes."

"And an ambulance brought me to… What is this place?"

"You're in Manhattan Hospital."

"Am I…am I badly hurt?" He hesitated, and she swallowed hard. "Please, tell me the truth. What kind of injuries do I have?"

"Some bruises. A cut above your eye…they had to put in stitches—"

"Why can't I remember anything? Do I have amnesia?"

She asked it matter-of-factly, as if she'd been inquiring about nothing more devastating than a common cold, but he wasn't a fool, she knew he could sense the panic that she fought to keep from her voice because the hands that still clasped her shoulders tightened again.

"The taxi only brushed you," he said. "But when you fell, you hit your head against the curb."

"My mind is like a—a blackboard that's been wiped clean. You keep calling me 'Joanna' but the name has no meaning to me. I don't know who 'Joanna' is."

Her eyes had grown accustomed to the shadowy darkness; she could almost see him clearly now. He had a hard face with strong features: a straight blade of a nose, a slash of a mouth, hair that looked to be thick and dark and perhaps a bit overlong.

"And me?" His voice had fallen to a whisper; she had to strain to hear it. "Do you know who I am, Joanna?"

She took a deep, shuddering breath. Should she remember him? Should she at least know his name?

"No," she said. "No. I don't."

There was a long, almost palpable silence. She felt the quick bite of his fingers into her flesh and then he lifted his hands away, carefully, slowly, as if she were a delicate glass figurine he'd just returned to its cabinet for fear a swift movement would make it shatter.

He rose slowly to his feet and now she could see that he was tall, that the broad shoulders were matched by a powerful chest that tapered to a narrow waist, slim hips and long, well-proportioned legs. He stood beside the bed looking down at her, and then he nodded and thrust his fingers through his hair in a gesture instinct told her was as familiar to her as it was habitual to him.

"The doctors told me to expect this," he said, "but..."

He shrugged so helplessly, despite the obvious power of his silhouette, that Joanna's heart felt his frustration.

"I'm sorry," she murmured. "I'm terribly, terribly sorry."

His smile was bittersweet. He sat down beside her again and took her hand in his. She had a fleeting memory, one that was gone before she could make sense of it. She saw his dark head bent over a woman's hand, saw his lips pressed to the palm...

Was the woman her? Was he going to bring her hand to his mouth and kiss it?

Anticipation, bright as the promise of a new day and sweet as the nectar of a flower, made her pulse-beat quicken. But all he did was lay her hand down again and pat it lightly with his.

"It isn't your fault, Joanna. There's nothing to apologize for."

She had the feeling that there was, that she owed him many apologies for many things, but that was silly. How could she owe anything to a man she didn't know?

"Please," she said softly, "tell me your name."

His mouth twisted. Then he rose to his feet, walked to the window and stared out into the night. An eternity seemed to pass before he turned and looked at her again.

"Of course." There was a difference in him now, in his tone and in the way he held himself, and it frightened her. "My name is David. David Adams."

Joanna hesitated. The black pit that had swallowed her so many times since the accident seemed to loom at her feet.

"David Adams," she murmured, turning the name over in her mind, trying—failing—to find in it some hint of familiarity. "We—we have the same last name."

He laughed, though there was no levity to it.

"I can see you haven't lost your talent for understatement, Joanna. Yes, we have the same last name."

"Are we related, then?"

His mouth twisted again, this time with a wry smile. "Indeed, we are, my love. You see, Joanna, I'm your husband."

CHAPTER TWO

THE nurses all knew him by name, but after ten days there was nothing surprising in that.

What was surprising, David thought as his driver competently snaked the Bentley through the crowded streets of midtown Manhattan, was that he'd become something of a celebrity in the hospital.

Morgana, his P.A., had laughed when he'd first expressed amazement and then annoyance at his star status.

"I'm not Richard Gere, for heaven's sake," he'd told her irritably after he'd been stopped half a dozen times for his autograph en route to Joanna's room. "What in hell do they want with the signature of a stodgy Wall Street banker?"

Morgana had pointed out that he wasn't just a Wall Street banker, he was the man both the President of the World Bank and the President of the United States turned to for financial advice, even though his politics were not known by either.

As for stodgy... Morgana reminded him that *CityLife* magazine had only last month named him to its list of New York's Ten Sexiest Men.

David, who'd been embarrassed enough by the designation so he'd done an admirable job of all but forgetting it, had flushed.

"Absurd of them to even have mentioned my name in that stupid article," he'd muttered, and Morgana, honest as always, had agreed.

The media thought otherwise. In a rare week of no news, an accident involving the beautiful young wife of New York's Sexiest Stockbroker was a four-star event.

The ghouls had arrived at the Emergency Room damned

near as fast as he had so that when he'd jumped from his taxi he'd found himself in a sea of microphones and cameras and shouted questions, some so personal he wouldn't have asked them of a close friend. David had clenched his jaw, ignored them all and shoved his way through the avaricious mob without pausing.

That first encounter had taught him a lesson. Now, he came and went by limousine even though he hated the formality and pretentiousness of the oversize car he never used but for the most formal business occasions. Joanna had liked it, though. She loved the luxury of the plush passenger compartment with its built-in bar, TV and stereo.

David's mouth twisted. What irony, that the car he disliked and his wife loved should have become his vehicle of choice, since the accident.

It had nothing to do with the bar or the TV. It was just that he'd quickly learned that the reporters who still hung around outside the hospital pounced on taxis like hyenas on wounded wildebeests. Arriving by limo avoided the problem. The car simply pulled up at the physicians' entrance, David stepped out, waved to the security man as if he'd been doing it every day of his life and walked straight in. The reporters had yet to catch on, though it wouldn't matter, after tonight. This would be his last visit to the hospital.

By this time tomorrow, Joanna would be installed in a comfortable suite at Bright Meadows Rehabilitation Center. The place had an excellent reputation, both for helping its patients recover and for keeping them safe from unwelcome visitors. Bright Meadows was accustomed to catering to high-profile guests. No one whose name hadn't been placed on an approved list would get past the high stone walls and there was even a helicopter pad on the grounds, if a phalanx of reporters decided to gather at the gates.

Hollister pulled up to the private entrance as usual and David waved to the guard as he walked briskly through the door and into a waiting elevator. He was on the verge of breathing a sigh of relief when a bottle blonde with a triumphant smile on her face and a microphone clutched in her hand sprang out of the shadows and into the elevator. She jammed her finger on the Stop button and turned up the wattage on her smile.

"Mr. Adams," she said, "millions of interested *Sun* readers want to know how Mrs. Adams is doing."

"She's doing very well, thank you," David said politely.

"Is she really?" Her voice dropped to a whisper that oozed compassion the same way a crocodile shed tears. "You can tell *Sun* readers the truth, David. What's the real extent of your wife's injuries?"

"Would you take your finger off that button, please, miss?" The blonde edged nearer. "Is it true she's in a coma?"

"Step back, please, and let go of that button."

"David." The blond leaned forward, her heavily kohled eyes, her cleavage and her microphone all aimed straight at him. "We heard that your wife's accident occurred while she was en route to the airport for your second honeymoon in the Caribbean. Can you confirm that for our readers?"

David's jaw tightened. He could sure as hell wipe that look of phony sympathy from the blonde's face, he thought grimly. All he had to do was tell her the truth, that Joanna had been on her way to the airport, all right, and then to the Caribbean—and to the swift, civilized divorce they had agreed upon.

But the last thing he'd ever do was feed tabloid gossip. His life was private. Besides, ending the marriage was out of the question now. He and Joanna were husband and wife, by license if not by choice. He would stand by her, provide the best care possible until she was well again...

"Mr. Adams?"

The blonde wasn't going to give up easily. She had rearranged her face so that her expression had gone from compassion to sincere inquiry. He thought of telling her that the last time he'd seen that look it had been on the face of a shark that had a sincere interest in one or more of his limbs while he'd been diving off the Mexican coast.

"I only want to help you share your problems with our readers," she said. "Sharing makes grief so much easier to bear, don't you agree?"

David smiled. "Well, Miss..."

"Washbourne." She smiled back, triumphant. "Mona Washbourne, but you can call me Mona."

"Well, Mona, I'll be happy to share this much." David's smile vanished as quickly as it had appeared. He raised his arm, shot back the cuff of his dark blue suit jacket, and looked at his watch. "Get that mike out of my face and your finger off that button in the next ten seconds or you're going to regret it."

"Is that a threat, Mr. Adams?"

"Your word, Mona, not mine."

"Because it certainly sounded like one. And I've got every word, right here, on my tape rec—"

"I never make threats, I only make promises. Anyone who's had any dealings with me can tell you that." His eyes met hers. "You're down to four seconds, and still counting."

Whatever Mona Washbourne saw in that cold, steady gaze made her jerk her finger from the Stop button and step out of the elevator.

"Didn't you ever hear of freedom of the press? You can't go around bullying reporters."

"Is that what you are?" David said politely. He punched the button for Joanna's floor and the doors began to shut. "A member of the press? Damn. And here I was, thinking you were a…"

The doors snapped closed. Just as well, he thought wearily, and leaned back against the wall. Insulting the Mona Washbournes of the world only made them more vicious, and what was the point? He was accustomed to pressure, it was part of the way he earned his living.

OK, so the last week and a half had been rough. Personally rough. He didn't love Joanna anymore, hell, he wasn't even sure if he had ever loved her to begin with, but that didn't mean he hadn't almost gone crazy with fear when the call had come, notifying him of the accident. He wasn't heartless. What man wouldn't react to the news that the woman he was married to had been hurt?

And, as it had turned out, "hurt" was a wild word to describe what had happened to Jo. David's mouth thinned. She'd lost her memory. She didn't remember anything. Not her name, not their marriage...

Not him.

The elevator doors opened. The nurse on duty looked up, frowning, an automatic reminder that it was past visiting hours on her lips, but then her stern features softened into a girlish smile.

"Oh, it's you, Mr. Adams. We thought you might not be stopping by this evening."

"I'm afraid I got tied up in a meeting, Miss Howell."

"Well, certainly, sir. That's what I told Mrs. Adams, that you were probably running late."

"How is my wife this evening?"

"Very well, sir." The nurse's smile broadened. "She's had her hair done. Her makeup, too. I suspect you'll find her looking more and more like her old self."

"Ah." David nodded. "Yes, well, that's good news."

He told himself that it was as he headed down the hall toward Joanna's room. She hadn't looked at all like herself since the accident.

"Why are you looking at me like that?" she'd asked him, just last evening, and when he hadn't answered, her hand had shot to her forehead, clamping over the livid, half-moon scar that marred her perfect skin. "It's ugly, isn't it?"

David had stood there, wanting to tell her that what he'd been staring at was the sight of a Joanna he'd all but forgotten, one who lent grace and beauty even to an undistinguished white hospital gown, who wore her dark hair loose in a curling, silken cloud, whose dark-lashed violet eyes were not just free of makeup but wide and vulnerable, whose full mouth was the pink of roses.

He hadn't said any of that, of course, partly because it was just sentimental slop and partly because he knew she wouldn't want to hear it. That Joanna had disappeared months after their wedding and the Joanna who'd replaced her was always careful about presenting an impeccably groomed self to him and to the world. So he'd muttered something about the scar being not at all bad and then he'd changed the subject, but he hadn't forgotten the moment.

It had left a funny feeling in his gut, seeing Joanna that way, as if a gust of wind had blown across a calendar and turned the pages backward. He'd mentioned it to Morgana in passing, not the clutch in his belly but how different Joanna looked and his Personal Assistant, with the clever, understanding instincts of one woman for another, had cluck-clucked.

"The poor girl," she'd said, "of course she looks different! Think what she's gone through, David. She probably dreads looking at herself in the mirror. Her cosmetic case and a visit from her hairdresser will go a long way toward cheering her spirits. Shall I make the arrangements?"

David had hesitated, though he couldn't imagine the reason. Then he'd said yes, of course, that he'd have done it himself, if he'd thought of it, and Morgana had smiled and said that the less men knew about women's desires to make themselves beautiful, the better.

So Morgana had made the necessary calls, and he'd seen to it that Joanna's own robes, nightgowns and slippers were packed by her maid and delivered to the hospital first thing this morning, and now, as he knocked and then opened the door of her room, he was not surprised to find the Joanna he knew waiting for him.

She was standing at the window, her back to him. She was dressed in a pale blue cashmere robe, her hair drawn back from her face and secured at the nape in an elegant knot. Her posture was straight and proud—or was there a curve to her shoulders and a tremble to them, as well?

He stepped inside the room and let the door swing shut behind him.

"Joanna?"

She turned at the sound of his voice and he saw that everything about her had gone back to normal. The vulnerability had left her eyes; they'd been done up in some way he didn't pretend to understand so that they were somehow less huge and far more sophisticated. The bright color had been toned down in her cheeks and her mouth, while still full and beautiful, was no longer the color of a rose but of the artificial blossoms only found in a lipstick tube.

The girl he had once called his Gypsy was gone. The stunning Manhattan sophisticate was back and it was stupid to feel a twinge of loss because he'd lost his Gypsy a long, long time ago.

"David," Joanna said. "I didn't expect you."

"I was stuck in a meeting... Joanna? Have you been crying?"

"No," she said quickly, "no, of course not. I just—I have a bit of a headache, that's all." She swallowed; he could see the movement of muscle in her long, pale throat. "Thank you for the clothes you sent over."

"Don't be silly. I should have thought of having your own things delivered to you days ago."

The tip of her tongue snaked across her lips. She looked down at her robe, then back at him.

"You mean...I selected these things myself?"

He nodded. "Of course. Ellen packed them straight from your closet."

"Ellen?"

"Your maid."

"My..." She gave a little laugh, walked to the bed and sat down on the edge of the mattress. "I have a maid?" David nodded. "Well, thank her for me, too, please. Oh, and thank you for arranging for me to have my hair and my makeup done."

"It isn't necessary to thank me, Joanna. But you're welcome."

He spoke as politely as she did, even though he had the sudden urge to tell her that he'd liked her better with her hair wild and free, with color in her cheeks that didn't come from a makeup box and her eyes dark and sparkling with laughter.

She was beautiful now but she'd been twice as beautiful before.

David frowned. The pressure of the past ten days was definitely getting to him. There was no point in remembering the past when the past had never been real.

"So," he said briskly, "are you looking forward to getting sprung from this place tomorrow?"

Joanna stared at him. She knew what she was supposed to say. And the prospect of getting out of the hospital had been exciting...until she'd begun to think about what awaited her outside these walls.

By now, she knew she and David lived in a town house near Central Park but she couldn't begin to imagine what sort of life they led. David was rich, that much was obvious, and yet she had the feeling she didn't know what it meant to lead the life of a wealthy woman.

Which was, of course, crazy, because she didn't know what it meant to lead any sort of life, especially one as this stranger's wife.

He was so handsome, this man she couldn't remember. So unabashedly male, and here she'd been lying around looking like something the cat had dragged in, dressed in a shapeless hospital gown with no makeup at all on her face and her hair wild as a whirlwind, and then her clothes and her hairdresser and her makeup had arrived and she'd realized that her husband preferred her to look chic and sophisticated.

No wonder he'd looked at her as if he'd never seen her before just last evening.

Maybe things would improve between them now. The nurses all talked about how lucky she was to be Mrs. David Adams. He was gorgeous, they giggled, so sexy...

So polite, and so cold.

The nurses didn't know that, but Joanna did. Was that how he'd always treated her? As if they were strangers who'd just met, always careful to do and say the right thing? Or was it the accident that had changed things between them? Was he so removed, so proper, because he knew she couldn't remember him or their marriage?

Joanna wanted to ask, but how could you ask such intimate things of a man you didn't know?

"Joanna, what's the matter?" She blinked and looked up at David. His green eyes were narrowed with concern as they met hers. "Have the doctors changed their minds about releasing you?"

Joanna forced a smile to her lips. "No, no, the cell door's still scheduled to open at ten in the morning. I was just thinking about...about how it's going to be to go...to go..." Home, she thought. She couldn't bring herself to say the word, but then, she didn't have to. She wasn't going home tomorrow, she was going to a rehab center. More white-tiled walls, more high ceilings, more brightly smiling nurses... "Where is Big Meadows, anyway?"

"Bright Meadows," David said, with a smile. "It's about an hour's drive from here. You'll like the place, Jo. Lots of trees, rolling hills, an Olympic-size swimming pool and there's even an exercise room. Nothing as high-tech as your club, I don't think, but even so—"

"My club?"

Damn, David thought, damn! The doctors had warned him against jogging her memory until she was ready, until she began asking questions on her own.

"Sorry. I didn't mean to—"

"Do I belong to an exercise club?"

"Well, yeah."

"You mean, one of those places where you dress up in a silly Spandex suit so you can climb on a treadmill to work up a sweat?"

David grinned. It was his unspoken description of the Power Place, to a tee.

"I think the Power Place would be offended to hear itself described in quite that way but I can't argue with it, either."

Joanna laughed. "I can't even imagine doing that. I had the TV on this morning and there was this roomful of people jumping up and down...they looked so silly, and now you're telling me that I do the same thing?"

"The Power Place," David said solemnly, "would definitely not like to hear you say that."

"Why don't I run outdoors? Or walk? Didn't you say I—we—live near Central Park?"

His smile tilted. It was as if she was talking about another person instead of herself.

"Yes. We live less than a block away. And I don't know why you didn't run there. I do, every morning."

"Without me?" she said.

"Yes. Without you."

"Didn't we ever run together?"

He stared at her. They had; he'd almost forgotten. She'd run right along with him the first few weeks after their marriage. They'd even gone running one warm, drizzly morning and had the path almost all to themselves. They'd been jogging along in silence when she'd suddenly yelled out a challenge and sped away from him. He'd let her think she was going to beat him for thirty or forty yards and then he'd put on some speed, come up behind her, snatched her into his arms and tumbled them both off the path and into the grass. He'd kissed her until she'd stopped laughing and gone soft with desire in his arms, and then they'd flagged a cab to take them the short block back home...

He frowned, turned away and strode to the closet. "You said you preferred to join the club," he said brusquely, "that it was where all your friends went and that it was a lot more pleasant and a lot safer to run on an indoor track than in the park. Have you decided what you're going to wear tomorrow?"

"But how could it be safer? If you and I ran together, I was safe enough, wasn't I?"

"It was better that way, Joanna. We both agreed that it was. My schedule's become more and more erratic. I have to devote a lot of hours to business. You know that. I mean, you don't know it, not anymore, but..."

"That's OK, you don't have to explain." Joanna smiled tightly. "You're a very busy man. And a famous one. The nurses all keep telling me how lucky I am to be married to you."

David's hand closed around the mauve silk suit hanging in the closet.

"They ought to mind their business," he said gruffly.

"Don't be angry with them, David. They mean well."

"Everybody ought to mind their damned business," he said, fighting against the rage he felt suddenly, inexplicably, rising within him. "The nurses, the reporters—"

"Reporters?"

For the second time that night, David cursed himself. He could hear the sudden panic in Joanna's voice and he turned and looked at her.

"Don't worry about them. I won't let them get near you."

"But why…" She stopped, then puffed out her breath. "Of course. They want to know about the accident, about me, because I'm Mrs. David Adams."

"They won't bother you, Joanna. Once I get you to Bright Meadows…"

"The doctors say I'll have therapy at Bright Meadows."

"Yes."

"What kind of therapy?"

"I don't know exactly. They have to evaluate you first."

"Evaluate me?" she said with a quick smile.

"Look, the place is known throughout the country. The staff, the facilities, are all highly rated."

Joanna ran the tip of her tongue across her lips. "I don't need therapy," she said brightly. "I just need to remember."

"The therapy will help you do that."

"How?" She tilted her head up. Her smile was brilliant, though he could see it wobble just a little. "There's nothing wrong with me physically, David. Or mentally. I don't need to go for walks on the arm of an aide or learn basket-weaving or—or lie on a couch while some doctor asks me silly questions about a childhood I can't remember."

David's frown deepened. She was saying the same things he'd said when Bright Meadows had been recommended to him.

"Joanna's not crazy," he'd said bluntly, "and she's not crippled."

The doctors had agreed, but they'd pointed out that there really wasn't anywhere else to send a woman with amnesia…unless, of course, Mr. Adams wished to take his wife home? She needed peaceful, stress-free surroundings and, at least temporarily, someone to watch out for her. Could a man who put in twelve-hour days provide that?

No, David had said, he could not. He had to devote himself to his career. He had a high-powered Wall Street firm to run and clients to deal with. Besides, though he didn't say so to the doctors, he knew that he and Joanna could never endure too much time alone together.

There was no question but that Bright Meadows was the right place for Joanna. The doctors, and David, had agreed.

Had Joanna agreed, too? He was damned if he could remember.

"David?"

He looked at Joanna. She was smiling tremulously.

"Couldn't I just...isn't there someplace I could go that isn't a hospital? A place I could stay, I mean, where maybe the things around me would jog my memory?"

"You need peace and quiet, Joanna. Our town house isn't—"

She nodded and turned away, but not before he'd seen the glitter of tears in her eyes. She was crying. Quietly, with great dignity, but she was crying all the same.

"Joanna," he said gently, "don't."

"I'm sorry." She rose quickly and hurried to the window where she stood with her back to him. "Go on home, please, David. It's late, and you've had a long day. The last thing you need on your hands is a woman who's feeling sorry for herself."

Had she always been so slight? His mental image of his wife was of a slender, tall woman with a straight back and straight shoulders, but the woman he saw at the window seemed small and painfully defenseless.

"Jo," he said, and he started slowly toward her, "listen, everything's going to be OK. I promise."

She nodded. "Sure," she said in a choked whisper.

He was standing just behind her now, close enough so that he could see the reddish glints in her black hair, so that he could almost convince himself he smelled the delicate scent of gardenia that had always risen from her skin until she'd changed to some more sophisticated scent.

"Joanna, if you don't like Bright Meadows, we'll find another place and—"

She spun toward him, her eyes bright with tears and with something else. Anger?

"Dammit, don't talk to me as if I were a child!"

"I'm not. I'm just trying to reassure you. I'll see to it you have the best of care. You know that."

"I don't know anything," she said, her voice trembling not with self-pity but yes, definitely, with anger. "You just don't understand, do you? You think, if you have them fix my hair and my face, and ship me my clothes and make me look like Joanna Adams, I'll turn into Joanna Adams."

"No," David said quickly. "I mean, yes, in a way. I'm trying to help you be who you are."

Joanna lifted her clenched fist and slammed it against his chest. David stumbled back, not from the blow which he'd hardly felt, but from shock. He couldn't remember Joanna raising her voice, let alone her hand. Well, yes, there'd been that time after they were first married, when he'd been caught late at a dinner meeting and he hadn't telephoned and she'd been frantic with worry by the time he came in at two in the morning...

"Damn you, David! I don't know who I am! I don't know this Joanna person." She raised her hand again, this time to punctuate each of her next words with a finger poked into his chest. "And I certainly don't know you!"

"What do you want to know? Ask and I'll tell you."

She took a deep, shuddering breath. "For starters, I'd like to know why I'm expected to believe I'm really your wife!"

David started to laugh, then stopped. She wasn't joking. One look into her eyes was proof of that. They had gone from violet to a color that was almost black. Her hands were on her hips, her posture hostile. She looked furious, defiant...and incredibly beautiful.

"What are you talking about?"

"What do you mean, what am I talking about? I said it

clearly enough, didn't I? You say I'm your wife, but I don't remember you. So why should I let you run my life?"

"Joanna, for heaven's sake—"

"Can you *prove* that we're married?"

David threw up his hands. "I don't believe this!"

"Can you prove it, David?"

"Of course I can prove it! What would you like to see? Our marriage license? The cards we both signed and mailed out last Christmas? Dammit, of course we're married. Why would I lie about such a thing?"

He wouldn't. She knew that, deep down inside, but that had nothing to do with this. She was angry. She was furious. Let *him* try waking up in a hospital bed without knowing who he was, let *him* try having a stranger walk in and announce that as of that moment, all the important decisions of your life were being taken out of your hands.

But most of all, let him deal with the uncomfortable feeling that the person you were married to had been a stranger for a long, long time, not just since you'd awakened with a lump on your head and a terrible blankness behind your eyes.

"Answer me, Joanna. Why in hell would I lie?"

"I don't know. I'm not even saying that you are. I'm just trying to point out that the only knowledge I have of my own identity is your word."

David caught hold of her shoulders. "My word is damned well all you need!"

It was, she knew it was. It wasn't just the things the nurses had said about how lucky she was to be the wife of such a wonderful man as David Adams. She'd managed to read a bit about him in a couple of old magazines she'd found in the lounge.

On the face of it, David Adams was Everywoman's Dream.

But she wasn't Everywoman. She was lost on a dark road without a light to guide her and the only thing she felt whenever she thought of herself as Mrs. David Adams was a dizzying sense of disaster mingled in with something else, something just as dizzying but also incredibly exciting.

It terrified her, almost as much as the lack of a past, yet

instinct warned that she mustn't let him know that, that the best defense against whatever it was David made her feel when he got too close was a strong offense, and so instead of backing down under his furious glare, Joanna glared right back.

"No," she said, "your word isn't enough! I don't know anything about you. Not anything, what you eat for breakfast or—or what movies you like to see or who chooses those—those stodgy suits you wear or—"

"Stodgy?" he growled. "Stodgy?"

"You heard me."

David stared down at the stranger he held clasped by the shoulders. Stodgy? Hell, for Joanna to use that word to describe him was ludicrous. She was right, she didn't know the first thing about him; they were strangers.

What she couldn't know was that it had been that way for a long time.

But not always. No, not always, he thought while his anger grew, and before he could think too much about what he was about to do, he hauled Joanna into his arms and kissed her.

She gave a gasp of shock and struggled against the kiss. But he was remorseless, driven at first by pure male outrage and then by the taste of her, a taste he had not known in months. The feel of her in his arms, the softness of her breasts against his chest, the long length of her legs against his, made him hard with remembering.

He fisted one hand in her hair, holding her captive to his kiss, while the other swept down and cupped her bottom, lifting her into his embrace, bringing her so close to him that he felt the sudden quickened beat of her heart, heard the soft little moan that broke in her throat as his lips parted hers, and then her arms were around his neck and she was kissing him back as hungrily as he was kissing her...

"Oh, my, I'm terribly sorry. I'll come back a bit later, shall I?"

They sprang apart at the sound of the shocked female voice. Both of them looked at the door where the night nurse stood staring at them, her eyes wide.

"I thought Mrs. Adams might want some help getting ready

for bed but I suppose...I mean, I can see..." The nurse blushed. "Has Mrs. Adams regained her memory?"

"Mrs. Adams is capable of being spoken to, not about," Joanna said sharply. Her cheeks colored but her gaze was steady. "And no, she has not regained her memory."

"No," David said grimly, "she has not." He stalked past the nurse and pushed open the door. "But she's going to," he said. "She can count on it."

CHAPTER THREE

ALL right. Ok. So he'd made an ass of himself last night.

David stood in his darkened kitchen at six o'clock in the morning and told himself it didn't take a genius to figure that much out.

Kissing Joanna, losing his temper...the whole thing had been stupid. It had been worse than stupid. Joanna wasn't supposed to get upset and he sure as hell had upset her.

So why hadn't he just gone home, phoned her room and apologized? Why couldn't he just mentally kick himself in the tail, then put what had happened out of his head?

They were all good questions. It was just too bad that he didn't have any good answers, and he'd already wasted half the night trying to come up with one.

He'd always prided himself on his ability to face a mistake squarely, learn from it, then put it behind him and move on.

That was the way he'd survived childhood in a series of foster homes, a double hitch in the Marines and then a four year scholarship at an Ivy League university where he'd felt as out of place as a wolf at a sheep convention.

So, why was he standing here, drinking a cup of the worst coffee he'd ever tasted in his life, replaying that kiss as if it were a videotape caught in a loop?

He made a face, dumped the contents of the pot and the cup into the sink, then washed them both and put them into the drainer. Mrs. Timmons, his cook cum housekeeper, would be putting in an appearance in half an hour.

Why should she have to clean up a mess that he'd made?

David opened the refrigerator, took out a pitcher of orange juice and poured himself a glass. You made a mess, you cleaned it up...which brought him straight back to why he was standing around here in the first place.

The unvarnished truth was that if he'd divorced Joanna sooner, he wouldn't be in this situation. By the time she'd stepped off that curb, she'd have been out of his life.

He'd known almost two years ago that he wanted out of the marriage, that the woman he'd taken as his wife had been nothing but a figment of his imagination. Joanna hadn't been a sweet innocent whose heart he'd stolen. She'd been a cold-blooded schemer who'd set out to snare a rich husband, and she'd succeeded.

Because it had taken him so damned long to admit the truth, he was stuck in this sham of a marriage for God only knew how much longer.

David slammed the refrigerator door shut with far more force than the job needed, walked to the glass doors that opened onto the tiny patch of green that passed for a private garden in midtown Manhattan, and stared at the early morning sky.

Corbett and his team of white-coated witch doctors wouldn't say how long it would take her to recover. They wouldn't even guarantee there'd be a recovery. The only thing they'd say was that she needed time.

"These things can't be rushed," Corbett had said solemnly. "Your wife needs a lot of rest, Mr. Adams. No shocks. No unpleasant surprises. That's vital. You do understand that, don't you?"

David understood it, all right. There was no possibility of walking into Joanna's room and saying, "Good evening, Joanna, and by the way, did I mention that we were in the middle of a divorce when you got hit by that taxi?"

Not that he'd have done it anyway. He didn't feel anything for Joanna, one way or another. Emotionally, mentally, he'd put her out of his life. Still, he couldn't in good conscience turn his back on her when she didn't even remember her own name.

When she didn't even remember him, or that she was his wife.

It was crazy, but as the days passed, that had been the toughest thing to take. It was one thing to want a woman out of your life but quite another to have her look at you blankly, or speak to you as if you were a stranger, her tone proper and always polite.

Until last night, when she'd suddenly turned on him in anger. And then he'd felt an answering anger rise deep inside himself, one so intense it had blurred his brain. What in hell had possessed him to haul her into his arms and kiss her like that? He'd thought she was going to slug him. What he'd never expected was that she'd turn soft and warm in his arms and kiss him back.

For a minute he'd almost forgotten that he didn't love her anymore, that she had never loved him, that everything he'd thought lay between them had been built on the quicksand of lies and deceit.

He turned away from the garden.

Maybe he should have listened to his attorney instead of the doctors. Jack insisted it was stupid to let sentiment get in the way of reality.

"So she shouldn't have any shocks," he'd said, "so big deal, she shouldn't have played you for a sucker, either. You want to play the saint, David? OK, that's fine. Pay her medical bills. Put her into that fancy sanitarium and shell out the dough for however long it takes for her to remember who she is. Put a fancy settlement into her bank account—but before you do any of that, first do yourself a favor and divorce the broad."

David had puffed out his breath.

"I hear what you're saying, Jack. But her doctors say—"

"Forget her doctors. Listen, if you want I can come up with our own doctors who'll say she's *non compos mentis* or that she's faking it and you're more than entitled to divorce her, if that's what's worrying you."

"Nothing's worrying me," David had replied brusquely. "I just want to be able to look at myself in the mirror. I survived four years being married to Joanna. I'll survive another couple of months."

Brave words, and true ones. David put his empty glass into

the dishwasher, switched off the kitchen light and headed through the silent house toward the staircase and his bedroom.

And survive he would. He understood Jack's concern but he wasn't letting Joanna back into his life, he was just doing what he could to ease her into a life of her own.

She didn't affect him anymore, not down deep where it mattered. The truth was that she never had. He'd tricked himself into thinking he'd loved her when actually the only part of his anatomy Joanna had ever reached was the part that had been getting men into trouble from the beginning of time...the part that had responded to her last night.

Well, there was no more danger of that. He wouldn't be seeing much of his wife after today. Once he'd driven her to Bright Meadows, that would be it. Except for paying the bills and a once-a-week visit, she'd be the problem of the Bright Meadows staff, not his.

Sooner or later, her memory would come back. And when it did, this pretense of a marriage would be over.

Joanna sat in the back of the chauffeured Bentley and wondered what Dr. Corbett would say if she told him she almost preferred being in the hospital to being in this car with her husband.

For that matter, what would her husband say?

She shot David a guarded look.

Not much, judging by his stony profile, folded arms and cold silence. From the looks of things, he wasn't any more pleased they were trapped inside this overstuffed living room on wheels than she was.

What a terrible marriage theirs must have been. Her throat constricted. Dr. Corbett had made a point of telling her that you didn't lose your intellect when you lost your memory. Well, you didn't lose your instincts, either, and every instinct she possessed told her that the marriage of Joanna and David Adams had not been a storybook love affair.

Was he like this with everyone, or only with her? He never seemed to smile, to laugh, to show affection.

Maybe that was why what had happened last night had been

such a shock. That outburst of raw desire was the last thing she'd expected. Had it been a rarity or was that the way it had been between them before the accident, polite tolerance interrupted by moments of rage that ended with her clinging to David's shoulders, almost pleading for him to take her, while the world spun out from beneath her feet?

She'd hardly slept last night. Even after she'd rung for the nurse and asked for a sleeping pill, she'd lain staring into the darkness, trying to imagine what would have happened if that passionate, incredible kiss hadn't been interrupted.

She liked to think she'd have regained her senses, pulled out of David's arms and slapped him silly.

But a sly whisper inside her head said that maybe she wouldn't have, that maybe, instead, they'd have ended up on the bed and to hell with the fact that the man kissing her was an absolute stranger.

Eventually, she'd tumbled into exhausted sleep only to dream about David stripping away her robe and nightgown, kissing her breasts and her belly and then taking her right there, on that antiseptically white hospital bed with her legs wrapped around his waist and her head thrown back and her sobs of pleasure filling the room.

A flush rose into Joanna's cheeks.

Which only proved how little dreams had to do with reality. David had apologized for his behaviour and she'd accepted the apology, but if he so much as touched her again, she'd—she'd—

"What's the matter?"

She turned and looked at him. He was frowning, though that wasn't surprising. His face had been set in a scowl all morning.

"Nothing," she said brightly.

"I thought I heard you whimper."

"Whimper? Me?" She laughed, or hoped she did. "No, I didn't...well, maybe I did. I have a, ah, a bit of a headache."

"Well, why didn't you say so?" He leaned forward and opened the paneled bar that was built into the Bentley. "Corbett gave you some pills, didn't he?"

"Yes, but I don't need them."

"Dammit, must you argue with me about everything?"

"I don't argue about everything...do I?"

David looked at her. She didn't. Actually, she never had. It was just this mood he was in this morning.

He sighed and shook his head. "Sorry. I guess I'm just feeling irritable today. Look, it can't hurt to take a couple of whatever he gave you, can it?"

"No, I suppose not."

He smiled, a first for the day that she could recall, poured her a tumbler of iced Perrier and handed it to her.

"Here. Swallow them down with this."

Joanna shook two tablets out of the vial and did as he'd asked.

"There," she said politely. "Are you happy now?"

It was the wrong thing to say. His brow furrowed instantly and his mouth took on that narrowed look she was coming to recognize and dislike.

"Since when did worrying about what makes me happy ever convince you to do anything?"

The words were out before he could call them back. Damn, he thought, what was the matter with him? A couple of hours ago, he'd been congratulating himself on his decision to play the role of supportive husband. Now, with at least half an hour's drive time to go, he was close to blowing the whole thing.

And whose fault was that? He'd walked into Joanna's room this morning and she'd looked at him as if she expected him to turn into a monster.

"I'm sorry about last night," he'd said gruffly, and she'd made a gesture that made it clear that what had happened had no importance at all...but she'd jumped like a scared cat when he'd tried to help her into the back of the car and just a couple of minutes ago, after sitting like a marble statue for the past hour, he'd caught her shooting him the kind of nervous look he'd always figured people reserved for vicious dogs.

Oh, hell, he thought, and turned toward her.

"Listen," he said, "about what happened last night..."

"I don't want to talk about it."

"No, neither do I. I just want to assure you it won't happen again."

"No," she said. Her eyes met his. "It won't."

"We've both been under a lot of pressure. The accident, your loss of memory…"

"What about before the accident?"

"What do you mean?"

Joanna hesitated. "I get the feeling that we…that we didn't have a very happy marriage."

It was his turn to hesitate now, but he couldn't bring himself to lie.

"It was a marriage," he said finally. "I don't know how to quantify it."

Joanna nodded. What he meant was, no, they hadn't been happy. It wasn't a surprise. Her husband didn't like her very much and she…well, she didn't know him enough to like him or dislike him, but it was hard to imagine she could ever have been in love with a man like this.

"Did Dr. Corbett tell you not to discuss our relationship with me? Whether it was good or not, I mean?"

"No," he said, this time with all honesty. "I didn't discuss our marriage with Corbett. Why would I?"

"I don't know. I just thought…" She sighed and tugged at the hem of her skirt. Not that there was any reason to. The hem fell well below her knees. "I just thought he might have asked you questions about—about us."

"I wouldn't have answered them," David said bluntly. "Corbett's a neurosurgeon, not a shrink."

"I know. I guess I've just got psychiatry on the brain this morning, considering where we're going."

"Bright Meadows? But I told you, it's a rehab center."

"Oh, I know that. I just can't get this weird picture out of my head. I don't know where it comes from but I keep seeing a flight of steps leading up to an old mansion with a nurse standing on top of the steps. She's wearing a white uniform and a cape, and she has—I know it's silly, but she has a mustache and buck teeth and a hump on her back."

David burst out laughing. "Cloris Leachman!"

"Who?"

"An actress. What you're remembering is a scene from an old movie with Mel Brooks called...I think it was *High Anxiety*. He played a shrink and she played—give me a minute— she played evil Nurse Diesel."

Joanna laughed. "Evil Nurse Diesel?"

"Uh-huh. We found the movie playing on cable late one night, not long after we met. We both said we didn't like Mel Brooks' stuff, slapstick comedy, but we watched for a few minutes and we got hooked. After a while, we were both laughing so hard we couldn't stop."

"Really?"

"Oh, yeah. We watched right to the end, and then I phoned around until I found an all-night place to order pizza and you popped a bottle of wine into the freezer to chill and then..." *And then I told you that I loved you and asked you to be my wife.*

"And then?"

David shrugged. "And then, we decided we'd give Mel Brooks' movies another chance." He cleared his throat. "It's got to be a good sign, that you remembered a movie."

She nodded. "A snippet of a movie, at least."

"Anyway, there's nothing to worry about." He reached out and patted her hand. "Believe me, you're not going to find anything like that waiting for you at Bright Meadows."

She didn't.

There was no nurse with a mustache and too many teeth waiting at the top of the steps. There were no dreary corridors or spaced-out patients wandering the grounds.

Instead, there was an air of almost manic cheer about the place. The receptionist smiled, the admitting nurse bubbled, the attendant who led them to a private, sun-drenched room beamed with goodwill.

"I just know you're going to enjoy your stay with us, Mrs. Adams," the girl said.

She sounds as if she's welcoming me to a hotel, Joanna

thought. But this isn't a hotel, it's a hospital, even if nobody calls it that, and I'm not sick. I just can't remember anything...

No. She couldn't think about that or the terror of it would rise up and she'd scream.

And she couldn't do that. She'd kept the fear under control until now, she hadn't let anyone see the panic that woke her in the night, heart pounding and pillow soaked with sweat.

Joanna turned toward the window and forced herself to take a deep, deep breath.

"Joanna?" David looked at the straight, proud back. A few strands of dark hair had come loose; they hung down against his wife's neck. He knew Joanna would fix it if she knew, that she'd never tolerate such imperfection. Despite the straightness of her spine, the severity of her suit, the tumble of curls lent her a vulnerability. He thought of how she'd once been...of how she'd once seemed.

All right, he knew that what she'd seemed had been a lie, that she wasn't the sweet, loving wife he'd wanted, but even so, she was in a tough spot now. It couldn't be easy, losing your memory.

He crossed the room silently, put his hands on her shoulders. He felt her jump beneath his touch and when he turned her gently toward him and she looked up at him, he even thought he saw her mouth tremble.

"Joanna," he said, his voice softening, "look, if you don't like this place, I'm sure there are others that—"

"This is fine," she said briskly.

He blinked, looked at her again, and knew he'd let his imagination work overtime. Her lips were curved in a cool smile and her eyes were clear.

David's hands fell to his sides. Whatever he'd thought he'd seen in her a moment ago had been just another example of how easily he could still be taken in, if not by his wife then by his own imagination.

"I'm sure I'm going to like it here," she said. "Now, if you don't mind terribly, I really would like to take a nap."

"Of course. I'd forgotten what an exhausting day this must have been for you." He started for the door. Halfway there, he paused and swung toward her. "I, uh, I'm not quite certain when I'll be able to get to see you again."

"Don't worry about it, David. This is a long way to come after a day's work and besides, I'm sure I'll be so busy I won't have time for visitors."

"That's exactly what I was thinking."

Joanna smiled. "Safe trip home," she said.

She held the smile until the door snicked shut after him. Then it dropped from her lips and she buried her face in her hands and wept.

Until today, she'd thought nothing could be as awful as waking up and remembering nothing about your life.

Now, she knew that it was even more horrible to realize that you were part of a loveless marriage.

"Mr. Adams?"

David looked up. He'd had his nose buried in a pile of reports he'd dredged out of the briefcase he always kept near at hand until the voice of his chauffeur intruded over the intercom.

"What is it, Hollister?"

"Sorry to bother you, sir, but I just caught a report on the radio about an overturned tractor trailer near the tunnel approach to the city."

David sighed and ran his hand through his hair. It wasn't any bother at all. The truth was, he didn't have the foggiest idea what was in the papers spread out on the seat beside him. He'd tried his damnedest to concentrate but that split instant when he'd seen those wispy curls lying against Joanna's pale skin kept intruding.

"Did they say anything about the traffic?"

"It's tied up for miles. Would you want me to take the long way? We could detour to the Palisades Parkway and take the bridge."

"Yes, that's a good idea, Hollister. Take the next turnoff and…" David frowned, then leaned forward. "No, the hell with that. Just pull over."

"Sir?"

"I said, pull over. Up ahead, where the shoulder of the road widens."

"Is there a problem, Mr. Adams?"

A taut smile twisted across David's mouth.

"No," he said, as the big car glided to a stop. "I just want to change seats with you."

"Sir?" Hollister said again. There was a world of meaning in the single word.

David laughed and jerked open the car door.

"I feel like driving, Hollister. You can stay up front, if you like. Just slide across the seat and put your belt on because I'm in the mood to see if this car can do anything besides look good."

For the first time in memory, Hollister smiled.

"She can do a lot besides look good, sir. She's not your Jaguar by a long shot but if you put your foot right to the floor, I think she'll surprise you."

David grinned. He waited until his chauffeur had fastened his seat belt and then he did as the man had suggested, put the car in gear and the pedal to the metal, and forgot everything but the road.

He called Joanna every evening, promptly at seven. Their conversations were always the same.

How was she? he asked.

Fine, she answered.

And how was she getting along at Bright Meadows?

She said "fine" to that one, too.

Friday evening, when he phoned, he told her he had some work to do Saturday but he'd see her on Sunday.

Only if he could fit it into his schedule, she said.

His teeth ground together at the polite distance in the words. Evidently, she didn't need to remember the past to know how she wanted to behave in the present.

"I'll be there," he said grimly, and hung up the phone.

Sunday morning, he went for his usual run. He showered, put on a pair of time-worn jeans, a pair of sneakers and—in deference to the warming Spring weather—a lightweight blue sweatshirt. Then he got behind the wheel of the Jaguar and drove upstate.

Halfway there, he realized that he was out of uniform. Joanna didn't care for the casual look. She didn't care for this car, either. She had, a long time ago. At least, she'd pretended she had.

The hell with it. It was too late to worry about and besides, it was one thing to pretend they hadn't been about to get divorced and quite another to redo his life. He'd done that for damned near four years and that had been three years and a handful of months too many.

The grounds of the rehab center were crowded with patients and visitors, but he spotted Joanna as soon as he drove through the gates. She was sitting on a stone bench beside a dogwood tree that was just coming into flower, the creamy blossoms a counterpoint to her dark hair. She was reading a book and oblivious to anything around her, which was typical of her. It was how she'd dealt with him during so much of the time they'd been married, as if she were living on a separate planet.

It made him furious, which was stupid, because he'd gotten over giving a damn about how she acted a long time ago. Still, after he'd parked the car and walked back to where she was sitting, he had to force himself to smile.

"Hi."

She looked up, her dark eyes wide with surprise.

"David!"

"Why so shocked?" He sat down beside her. "I told you I'd be here today."

"Well, I know what you said, but..."

But he hadn't cared enough to come up all week. Not that it mattered to her if she saw him or not...

"But?"

Joanna shut the book and put it on the bench beside her. "Nothing," she said. "I guess you just caught me by surprise."

He waited for her to say something more. When she didn't, he cleared his throat.

"So, how are things going? Have you settled in?"

"Oh, yes. Everyone's very nice."

"Good. And are they helping you?"

"Have I remembered, do you mean?" Joanna got to her feet and he rose, too. They began walking slowly along a path that wound behind the main building. "No, not a thing. Everyone tells me to be patient."

"But it's hard."

"Yes." She looked up at him. "For you, too."

He knew he was supposed to deny it, but he couldn't.

"Yes," he said quietly, "for me, too."

Joanna nodded. "I just can't help wondering..."

"What?"

She shook her head. She'd promised herself not to say anything; the words had just slipped out.

"Nothing."

"Come on, Joanna, you were going to ask me something. What is it?"

"Well, I know I'm not a doctor or anything, but—" She hesitated. "Wouldn't my memory come back faster if I were in familiar surroundings?" He looked at her, saying nothing, and she spoke more quickly. "You don't know what it's like, David, not to be able to picture your own house. The furniture, or the colors of the walls..."

"You want to come home," he said.

Joanna looked up at him. There was no mistaking the sudden flatness in his voice.

"I just want to get my memory back," she said softly. "It's what you want, too, isn't it?"

A muscle flickered in his jaw. "It wouldn't work," he said carefully. "You need peace and quiet, someone to look after you. I'm hardly ever home before ten at night and even when I am, the phone's forever ringing, and the fax is going..."

A cold hand seemed to clamp around her heart.

"I understand," she said.

"Who would take care of you? I could hire a nurse, yes, but—"

"I don't need anyone to take care of me." Her voice took on an edge. "I'm an amnesiac, not an invalid."

"Well, I know, but what about therapy?"

"What about it?" she said with sudden heat. "I don't see how learning to paint by numbers or weave baskets is going to help my memory."

David stopped and clasped her shoulders. He turned her toward him.

"You don't really weave baskets, do you?"

She sighed. "No, not really."

"Good." A grin twitched across his mouth. "For a minute there, I thought Nurse Diesel might be breathing down our necks."

Joanna's mouth curved. "Don't even mention that movie when you're here," she said in an exaggerated whisper. "They've got no sense of humor when it comes to things like that."

He laughed. "You said something?"

"Sure. The first day, an aide came to call for me. She said she was taking me to physical therapy and we got into this old, creaky elevator and headed for the basement. 'So,' I said, when the doors finally wheezed open, 'is this where you guys keep the chains and cattle prods?'" Joanna's eyes lit with laughter. "I thought she was going to go bonkers. I got a five minute lecture on the strides that have been made in mental health, blah, blah, blah..."

"Thanks for the warning."

"My pleasure."

They smiled at each other and then David cleared his throat, took Joanna's elbow politely, and they began walking again.

"What kind of therapy are you getting?"

"Oh, this and that. You can paint or sculpt in clay, and there's an hour of exercise in the pool and then a workout in the gym under the eye of a physical therapist—"

"Yeah, but there's nothing wrong with you physically."

"It's just the way things are done here. There's a routine and you follow it. Up at six, breakfast at six-thirty. An hour of painting or working with clay and then an hour in the pool before your morning appointment with your shrink."

"You see a psychiatrist, too?"

"Yes."

"Why?"

She made a face. "So far, to talk about how I'm going to adapt to my loss of memory. It didn't go over so well when I said I didn't want to adapt, that I wanted to get my memory back." She laughed. "Now I think the doctor's trying to figure why I'm always so hostile."

"That's ridiculous."

"Well, I said so, too, but she said—"

"I'll speak to the Director, Joanna. Someone must have forgotten to read your chart. You're not here for psychiatric counseling or for physical therapy, you're here to regain your memory."

"Don't waste your breath." Joanna stepped off the path. David watched her as she kicked off her shoes and sank down on the grass. "Mmm," she said, leaning back on her hands, tilting her face up and closing her eyes, "doesn't the sun feel wonderful?"

"Wonderful," he said, while he tried to figure out if he'd ever before seen her do anything so out of character. Did she know she was probably going to get grass stains on her yellow silk skirt? He kicked off his sneakers and sat down beside her. "What do you mean, don't waste my breath?"

"I already spoke to the Director. And he said since nobody knew much about amnesia and since I was here, the best thing I could do would be to put myself in their hands. I suppose it makes sense."

David nodded. "I suppose."

Joanna opened her eyes and smiled at him. "But I swear, if Nurse Diesel comes tripping into the room, I'll brain her with a raffia basket."

It stayed with him as he made the drive home.

Nurse Diesel.

It was a joke. He knew that. Bright Meadows was state of the art. It was about as far from a snake pit as you could get. The staff was terrific, the food was good—Joanna had joked that she'd already gained a pound though he couldn't see where. And what was wrong with spending some quiet time talking to a psychiatrist? And for the pool and all the rest…for a woman who used to spend half her day sweating on the machines at a trendy east side gym, physical therapy was a cinch.

His hands tightened on the wheel of the Jag.

But what did any of that have to do with helping her recover from amnesia? And that was the bottom line because until Joanna got her memory back, his life was stuck on hold.

Wouldn't my memory come back faster in familiar surroundings?

Maybe. On the other hand, maybe not. The last thing he wanted was to move his wife back into his life again, even if it was only on a temporary basis.

Besides, what he'd said about the house in Manhattan was true. It was nothing like Bright Meadows, with its big lawn, its sun-dappled pond, its bright rooms…

The house in Connecticut had all that, the lawns, the pond, the big, bright rooms. It had peace and quiet, birds singing in the gardens, it had everything including things that might stimulate Joahna's memory. They'd spent the first months of their marriage there and the days had been filled with joy and laughter…

Forget that. It was a stupid thought. He couldn't commute to the office from there, it was too far, even if he'd wanted to give it a try, which he didn't. He hated that damned house.

Joanna was better off where she was.

David stepped down harder on the gas.

She was much better off, and if that last glimpse he'd had of her as he left stayed with him for a couple of hours, so what? It had just been a trick of the light that seemed to have put the glint of tears in her eyes as she'd waved goodbye.

Even if it wasn't the light, what did he care?

He drove faster.

What in bloody hell did he care?

He drove faster still, until the old Jag was damned near flying, and then he muttered a couple of words he hadn't used since his days in the Corps, swerved the car onto the grass, swung it into a hard U-turn and headed back to Bright Meadows to tell his wife to pack her things, dump them into the back of the car and climb into the seat next to him so he could take her home.

Home to New York, because there wasn't a way in the world he would ever again take the almost ex-Mrs. Adams to Connecticut.

Not in this lifetime.

CHAPTER FOUR

IT STARTED raining, not long after David drove away from Bright Meadows for the second time.

He turned on the windshield wipers and Joanna listened to them whisper into the silence. The sound of the rain on the canvas roof and the tires hissing on the wet roadway was almost enough to lull her into a false sense of security.

Home. David was taking her home.

It was the last thing she'd ever expected, considering his reaction each time she'd suggested it, but now it was happening.

She was going home.

It was hard to believe that she'd stood on the lawn at Bright Meadows only a couple of hours ago, staring after David's car as it sped out the gate, telling herself that it was stupid to cry and stupider still to think that it wasn't her recovery he'd been thinking about when he'd insisted she was better off at the rehab center as much as it was the desire to keep her out of his life.

Why would her husband want to do that?

Before she'd even thought of an answer, she'd seen his car coming back up the drive. He'd pulled over, told her in brusque tones that he'd reconsidered what she'd said and that he'd decided she was right, she might get her memory back a lot faster if she were in familiar surroundings.

Joanna had felt almost giddy with excitement, even though he'd made it sound as if the change in plans was little more than an updated medical prescription.

"You go and pack," he'd said briskly, "while I do whatever needs doing to check you out of this place."

Before she knew it, she was sitting beside him on the worn leather seat of the aged sports car as it flew along the highway toward home.

Whatever that might be like.

A shudder went through her. David looked at her. Actually, he wasn't so much looking at her as he was glowering. Her stomach clenched. Was he already regretting his decision?

"Are you cold, Joanna?"

"No," she said quickly, "not a bit." She tried hard to sound bright and perky. "I'm just excited."

"Well, don't get too excited. Corbett wouldn't approve if your blood pressure shot up."

He smiled, to make it clear he was only joking. Joanna smiled back but then she locked her hands together in her lap.

"You don't have to worry," she said quietly. "I'm not going to be a burden to you."

"I never suggested you would be."

"Well, no, but I want to be sure we have this straight. I'm not sick, David."

"I know that."

"And I'm not an invalid. I'm perfectly capable of taking care of myself."

He sighed and shifted his long legs beneath the dash.

"Did I ever say you weren't?"

"I just want to be sure you understand that you're not going to have to play nursemaid."

"I'm not concerned about it," he said patiently. "Besides, there'll be plenty of people to look after you."

"I don't need looking after." She heard the faint edge in her words and she took a deep breath and told herself to calm down. "You won't have to hire a nurse or a companion or whatever."

"Well, we'll try it and see how it goes."

"It'll go just fine. I'm looking forward to doing things for myself."

"As long as you don't push too hard," he said. "I want you to promise to take it easy for a week or two."

"I will." Joanna looked down at her folded hands. "Thank you," she said softly.

"For what?"

"For changing your mind and agreeing to take me...to take me home."

He shrugged his shoulders. "There's no need to thank me. The more I thought about it, the more sensible it seemed. Anyway, I knew it was what you wanted."

But not what he wanted. The unspoken words hung in the air between them. After a moment, Joanna sighed.

"Is it much farther?"

"Only another half hour or so." He glanced over at her. "You look exhausted, Jo. Why don't you put your head back, close your eyes and rest for a while?"

"I'm not tired, I'm just..." She stopped in midsentence. How stupid she was. David's suggestion had been meant as much for himself as for her. He might be taking her home but he didn't have to spend an hour and a half trying to make polite conversation. "You're right," she said, and shot him a quick smile, "I think I will."

Joanna lay her head back and shut her eyes. This was better anyway, not just for him but for her. Let him think she was tired. Otherwise, she might just blurt out the truth.

The closer they got to their destination, the more nervous she felt.

Nervous? She almost laughed.

Be honest, she told herself. You're terrified.

All her babbling about wanting to go home was just that. What good could come of returning to a house she wouldn't recognize with a man she didn't know?

Mars might be a better place than "home."

She looked at David from beneath the sweep of her lashes. Oh, that rigid jaw. Those tightly clamped lips. The hands, white-knuckled on the steering wheel.

She wasn't the only one with second thoughts. It was clear that her husband regretted his spur-of-the-moment decision, too.

Why? Had their marriage really been so awful? It must have

been. There was no other way to explain the way he treated her, the careful politeness, the distant, unemotional behavior.

The only real emotion he'd shown her had been the night in her hospital room, when he'd kissed her.

The memory made her tingle. That kiss...that passionate, angry kiss. It had left her shaken, torn between despising his touch and the almost uncontrollable desire to go into his arms and give herself up to the heat.

Joanna's breath hitched. What was the matter with her? She'd been so caught up in wanting to go home that she hadn't given a moment's thought to what it might really mean. She and David were husband and wife. Did he expect...would he expect her to...? He hadn't so much as touched her since that night in the hospital, not even to kiss her cheek. Surely, he didn't think...

She shivered.

"Jo? What is it?"

She sat up straight, looked at David, then fixed her eyes on the ribbon of road unwinding ahead.

"I...I think you're right. I am feeling a little cold."

"I'll turn on the heat." He reached for a knob on the dashboard. "You always said that the heating system in this old heap was better suited to polar bears than people."

"Did I?" She smiled and stroked her hand lightly over the seat. "Actually, I can't imagine I ever said an unkind word about this beautiful old car."

He looked over at her. "Beautiful?"

"Mmm. What kind is it, anyway? A Thunderbird? A Corvette?"

"It's a '60 Jaguar XK 150," he said quietly.

"Ah," she said, her smile broadening, "an antique. Have you had it long?"

"Not long." His tone was stilted. "Just a few years."

"It must take lots of work, keeping an old car like this."

"Yeah." His hands tightened on the steering wheel. "Yeah, it does."

Her fingers moved across the soft leather again. "I'll bet you don't trust anybody to work on it."

David shot her a sharp look. "What makes you say that?"

"I don't know. It just seems logical. Why? Am I wrong?"

"No." He stared out at the road, forcing himself to concentrate on the slick asphalt. "No, you hit it right on the head. I do whatever needs doing on this car myself."

"Untouched by human hands, huh?" she said with a quick smile.

A muscle knotted in his jaw. "Somebody else who worked on the car with me used to say that, a long time ago."

"A super-mechanic, I'll bet."

"Yeah," he said briskly, "something like that." There was a silence and then he shifted his weight in his seat. "Will you look at that rain? It's coming down in buckets."

Joanna sighed. For a minute or two, it had looked as if they were going to have a real conversation.

"Yes," she said, "it certainly is."

David nodded. "Looks like the weatherman was wrong, as usual."

Such banal chitchat, Joanna thought, but better by far than uncomfortable silence.

"Still," she said brightly, "that's good, isn't it? One of the nurses was saying that it had been a dry Spring."

David sprang on the conversational lifeline as eagerly as she had.

"Dry isn't the word for it. The tulips in the park barely bloomed. And you know those roses you planted three summers ago? The pink ones? They haven't even…"

"I planted roses? I thought you said we lived in New York."

"We do." His hands tightened on the wheel. "But we have another place in…" His words trailed off in midsentence. "Hell," he muttered, "I'm sorry, Jo. I keep putting my foot in it today. I shouldn't have mentioned the damned roses or the house."

"Why not?"

"What do you mean, why not?" He glared at her. "Because you can't possibly remember either one, that's why not."

"That doesn't mean you shouldn't talk about them. If we're

going to avoid mention of anything I might not remember, what will there be left to talk about? Nothing but the weather," Joanna said, answering her own question, "and not even we can talk about the possibility of rain all the time."

"I suppose you're right."

"Of course I'm right! I don't expect you to censor everything you say. Besides, maybe it'll help if we—if you talk about the past."

"I just don't want to put any pressure on you, Joanna. You know what the doctors advised, that it was best to let your memory come back on its own."

"If it comes back at all." She flashed him a dazzling smile, one that couldn't quite mask the sudden tremor in her voice. "They also said there were no guarantees."

"You're going to be fine," he said with more conviction than he felt.

Joanna turned on him in sudden fury. "Don't placate me, David. Dropping platitudes all over the place isn't going to..." The rush of angry words stuttered to a halt. "Sorry," she whispered. "I didn't mean..."

A jagged streak of lightning lit the road ahead. The rain, which had been a steady gray curtain, suddenly roared against the old car. Fat drops, driven by the wind, flew through Joanna's window. She grabbed for the crank but it wouldn't turn. David made a face. He reached across her, grasped it and forced it to move.

"Got to fix that thing," he muttered. "Sorry."

Joanna nodded. She was sorry, he was sorry. They were so polite, like cautious acquaintances. But they weren't acquaintances, they were husband and wife.

Dear heaven, there was something terribly wrong in this relationship.

Her throat tightened. Whatever had possessed her to want to go home with this man?

She turned her face to the rain-blurred window and wished she had stayed at Bright Meadows. It hadn't been home, but at least it had been safe.

*   *   *

David looked at his wife, then at the road.

Well, he thought, his hand tightening on the steering wheel, wasn't that interesting?

His soft-spoken, demure wife had shown her temper again. A faint smile touched his lips.

Four years ago, that quick, fiery display wouldn't have surprised him. Not that the Joanna he'd married had been bad-tempered. She just hadn't been afraid to let her emotions show. In his world, where people seemed to think that sort of thing wasn't proper, his wife's willingness to show her feelings had been refreshing and endearing.

Not that it had lasted. Not that it could. David's hands clamped more tightly on the steering wheel. It had been a pose. His beloved wife had worn a mask to win his heart and once she'd decided it was safe to let it slip, she had.

As Morgana had pointed out, no one could keep up the innocent act forever.

He just wished to hell he knew who this was, seated beside him. This Joanna wasn't the woman he'd married nor the one he was divorcing. Everything about her was so familiar... And so unfamiliar. He'd known it ever since she'd regained consciousness after the accident, but he was uncomfortably aware of it today, starting with the minute she'd walked to the Jag to start the trip home.

He'd waited for her to make a face and ask where the Bentley was but she hadn't. Well, why would she? he'd reminded himself; she didn't remember how she'd felt about either car.

What he hadn't expected was the way she'd smiled when she'd settled in beside him, how she'd asked if the car really could go as fast as it looked. And then all those musings about how he probably never let anyone but him work on it.

That had struck too close to home. The Jag had been their project. They'd bought it together, tackled its restoration together, Joanna learning as fast as he could teach her until she was damned near as good at puttering under the hood as he was.

A bittersweet memory sprang into his head. They'd spent the week in Connecticut. He'd been called back to the city on business that he'd disposed of in record time and he'd gotten back to the house early, to find Joanna bent over the Jag's engine with her coverall-clad bottom in the air.

"Oh, David," she'd said, laughing as he'd grabbed her and whirled her around, "I was going to surprise you with this new—"

He'd never let her finish the sentence. He'd kissed her instead, and swung her up into his arms and carried her to their bedroom where he'd stripped away the bulky coverall to find her wearing nothing underneath but a tiny pair of white lace panties that he'd eased down her long, lovely legs...

He glanced over at those legs now. Her skirt had climbed up during the drive so that it was mid-thigh. She hadn't thought to adjust it. She hadn't thought to adjust her hair, either; the wind had tugged several strands loose from their moorings of pins and lacquer so that dark wisps curled sexily against her throat. David's gaze drifted lower. The quick burst of raindrops had dampened her silk blouse, the chill kiss of it tightening her nipples so they thrust against the fabric.

The Joanna he knew would have surely been aware of that. She would have fixed her hair, tugged down her skirt, crossed her arms over her breasts if she'd had to, done whatever it took to keep him from noticing that she was female, that she had sexual reactions if not sexual instincts.

David forced all his powers of concentration back to the rain-slicked road.

He had to stop thinking of Joanna as if she weren't Joanna. She had lost her memory but he had not lost his. He knew her. He knew the real woman.

And he had the increasingly uncomfortable feeling that he should have left her back at Bright Meadows, where she belonged.

The city glittered beneath the rain. It was beautiful, Joanna thought, and there was a vague familiarity to it the way there is to a place you've never visited but only seen in photographs.

David gave her a comforting smile.

"Just another couple of blocks," he said.

She nodded. Her hands lay in her lap, so tightly clasped that she could feel her nails digging into her flesh.

Would she recognize something? Would there be a moment when her memory would come rushing back?

In a movie, perhaps. But this was the real world, not one played out on the silver screen. The car made its way through clots of heavy traffic, turned onto Fifth Avenue, then down a side street. It was quiet here, the curb lined with plane trees in leaf, the town houses shouldering against each other in a way that spoke of money, power and elegant antiquity.

David pulled the car to the curb and shut off the engine. Joanna stared blankly at a building she had never seen before.

She'd asked him to tell her about their house when they'd first set out from Bright Meadows. Now, she could see that he'd described the place right down to the last detail. There was the gray stone facade and the windows with their black shutters; there were the black wrought-iron banisters and the stone steps leading to the front door.

Her stomach knotted in panic. "David," she said, swinging toward him…

But he'd already opened the car door and stepped out into the pouring rain.

"Stay put," he said, raising his voice over the deluge. "I'll go inside and get an umbrella and then I'll put the car away."

She flung her door open and got out. "No. No, wait…"

Her voice died away and she stood staring at the house, oblivious to the cold beat of the rain.

This is our home, she thought, mine and David's.

Her stomach twisted tighter. I want to go back to Bright Meadows, she thought desperately, oh, please…

"Dammit, Jo, what are you doing?"

David's voice broke through her frantic thoughts. He put his arm around her waist and began urging her forward.

"Come inside," he growled, "before you're soaked to the skin!"

She shook her head and pulled back against the tug of his arm. She didn't want to go into that house. She hated this place, *hated* it!

"For god's sake," David muttered, and he swung her into his arms. Caught off balance, she had no choice but to fling her arms around his neck.

Time seemed to stand still. The wet street, the rain... everything faded to insignificance. She was aware only of the feel of her husband's hard shoulders as she clutched them, the warmth of his powerful body against hers.

His eyes met hers; his arms tightened around her...

The door to the house swung open. "Sir," a voice said, "we had no idea..."

The moment of awareness shattered. "No," David said coolly, as he strode up the steps, "neither did I."

A tall, spare man with thinning hair stood in the doorway. Joanna recognized him as the chauffeur who'd driven her to Bright Meadows. Now, seeing him at the entrance to the town house, her mouth fell open in surprise.

"That's the limousine driver," she whispered to David. "What's he doing here?"

"His name is Hollister, Joanna. He lives here."

"Lives here?" she repeated stupidly.

"Madam," Hollister said, inclining his head as David moved past him, "welcome home."

"Hollister," David said, "is our chauffeur."

"You mean...that huge car we took to Bright Meadows belongs to us?"

"It does. Hollister drives it." He shot the man a wry smile. "And when he's not driving the Bentley, he's our butler."

"Our butler?" Joanna said, even more stupidly, craning her neck for a last glimpse of Hollister's bony, expressionless face. "David." Her voice fell to a whisper. "David, please, put me—"

"How do you do, madam."

A stern-faced woman in a dark dress stepped out of the gloomy darkness of the oak-paneled foyer.

"And this," David said, "is Mrs. Timmons. Our house-keeper."

A housekeeper, too? Joanna forced a smile to her lips.

"Hello, Mrs. Timmons." She bent her head toward David

and this time there was an urgency to her whispered words. "David, really, what will they think? If you'd just put me down—"

"And that," David said, as he started up a flight of long stairs, "is Ellen."

Joanna caught a flash of ruffled white apron, red hair and wide blue eyes.

"Madam," a girlish voice said shyly.

"Ellen," Joanna repeated numbly. She stared over David's shoulder as Ellen smiled and bobbed a curtsy. *A curtsy?* Did people really still do such things?

"A butler? A housekeeper? And a maid?" she whispered incredulously as they reached the second floor hall. "Do all those people really work for us?"

David smiled tightly. "You might say that."

"What do you mean, I might say…"

"Except for Mrs. Timmons, it's probably more accurate to say that the staff is yours." He shouldered open a door, stepped through it, and hit the light switch on the wall beside him with his elbow. "The staff," he said, lowering her to her feet, "and this bedroom."

Whatever questions Joanna had intended to ask flew out of her head as she stared in disbelief at her surroundings.

Last night she'd watched a program on television at Bright Meadows, something about Versailles or Fontainebleau; one of the glittering French palaces. Now, she wished she'd paid closer attention.

Whoever had designed this room must have taken their cue from a palace. The walls were covered with cream silk that matched the drapes at the windows and the coverings and hangings on the canopied bed. The floor was laid with richly patterned rugs. The furniture was white brushed with gold, except for a mirrored vanity table on the opposite wall. Its glass surface was covered with an assortment of stoppered bottles and jars, enough to stock a cosmetics shop.

The room was feminine and deeply sensual…and yet it wasn't. It was like a stage set; Joanna had the feeling that if she looked behind the walls and the furniture, she'd find out they were made of painted canvas.

She turned toward David in bewilderment. "This can't be my room."

He looked at her, his expression unreadable. "It is, I assure you. Now, get out of that wet dress while I go and get Ellen."

"No. I mean, I'd rather you didn't. I need a couple of minutes to…to…" She gave a hesitant laugh. "David, are you sure this room is…?"

He smiled sardonically. "It certainly isn't mine. I'm afraid vanities and frills aren't my style."

"You mean, we don't share a…"

She caught herself before the next word had tumbled out but it was too late. David's expression changed; she saw it before he turned away.

"No," he said. "We don't."

"Oh."

Oh? she thought, staring after him as he went into the adjoining bathroom. She'd just found out that she slept in a room only Marie Antoinette would have envied, that she and her husband didn't share a bedroom, and "Oh" was all she could manage?

Not that that part disappointed her. Sharing a room with a stranger wasn't what she wanted at all, it was only that the news had caught her by surprise…

"I've started the water in the tub."

She looked up. She could hear the water thundering in the bathroom as David came toward her. He'd pushed up the sleeves of his blue shirt; his forearms were muscled and tanned and dusted with dark hair.

"Joanna? I said—"

"I heard you." She cleared her throat. "Thank you."

"There's nothing to thank me for. Running a bath doesn't take any great effort."

"I meant…thank you for what you've done. For bringing me…home."

"Don't be silly," he said briskly. "You've every right to

be here. Now, come on. Get out of those wet things and into a hot tub.''

"David..." She reached out and put her hand lightly on his arm. "I know this isn't easy for either one of us. But I...I'm sure that my memory will come back soon."

His muscles tightened under her fingers. "Are you saying things seem familiar?"

"No," she admitted, "not yet. But they will. They have to," she said, with just a hint of desperation. "My memory will come back and then you and I can go back to living our normal lives."

David's eyes, as deep and as green as a winter sea, met hers.

"Our normal lives," he said.

"Yes." She gave a forced little laugh. "Whatever that may mean."

A muscle knotted in his jaw. For just a moment, she was certain he was going to say something, something she didn't think she wanted to hear, but the seconds ticked away and then he nodded.

"Of course," he said politely. "Now go on, take your bath. I'll tell Mrs. Timmons to make you a light supper and serve you here, on a tray."

"Alone, you mean?"

"I think it's best, don't you? I have some work to do and this way you can just get out of the tub, put on a robe and relax."

Joanna felt the sharp prick of tears behind her eyes, and felt immeasurably silly.

She was home, which was what she'd wanted, and her husband had shown nothing but kindness and consideration. He'd carried her up the stairs, drawn her bath and now he was offering her the chance to end the day quietly...

"Joanna?"

She looked up and smiled brightly. "That's very thoughtful of you, David. Yes, please, if you don't mind I think I'd like to have my supper alone. I'm...I'm awfully tired. You understand."

"Of course." He walked to the door and looked back at her, his hand on the knob. "I'll see you in the morning, then."

"In the morning," she said, "sure."

She held her bright smile until the door had shut after him. Then she walked slowly into the bathroom, sat down on the edge of the oversize circular tub and shut off the taps. The air was steamy, almost thick, and all at once the tears she'd fought against moments ago flooded her eyes and streamed down her face.

David was everything a woman could hope for.

But he wanted nothing to do with her. He didn't love her. He didn't even like her. She was not welcome in this house or in his life.

And she had absolutely no idea why.

CHAPTER FIVE

JOANNA had told David she'd see him the next morning, but he was gone by the time she came down the stairs at eight o'clock.

That was fine. The last thing she wanted to do was try and make small talk on her first day in this unfamiliar place that seemed more like a museum than a home.

She had breakfast under the cool, watchful eye of Mrs. Timmons, who seemed to offer silent disapproval of a meal made up of half a grapefruit and a cup of black coffee. Then she wandered from room to room, waiting for something to strike a familiar chord.

Nothing did.

At noon, as she was sitting in solitary splendor at a dining room table designed to seat twelve, David telephoned.

Hollister brought her the telephone.

How was she feeling? David asked politely. Did she need anything?

Joanna looked around her. A crown and a scepter, she thought, suppressing a rise of hysterical laughter.

"Don't worry about me," she said, very calmly, "I'm fine."

The conversation took no more than a minute. When it ended, Hollister gave a little bow and took the phone away. Mrs. Timmons marched in after him, bearing a huge lobster salad.

"You used to like this," she said in a crisp, no-nonsense voice, "or aren't I supposed to mention that kind of stuff?"

The frank, unsmiling face and blunt words were as out of

place in this elegant setting as they were welcome. Joanna smiled.

"Mention whatever you wish," she said, "otherwise I'm liable to end up biting into cardboard, just to find out if it was ever to my taste."

The housekeeper almost smiled. "Fine," she said, and clomped out.

After lunch, Joanna went outside and sat in the pocket garden behind the house. It was a sad, forlorn little place with one scrawny maple doing its best to survive.

Just like me, she thought, and she shuddered and went back inside and up to her room. She napped, woke up and read a magazine, then wandered through the rooms some more.

Mrs. Timmons was in the kitchen, slicing vegetables at the sink.

"Anything I can do to help?" Joanna asked from the doorway.

The housekeeper looked at her as if she were suffering not just from amnesia but from insanity.

"No, thank you, madam," she said, and went back to her work.

At six, David phoned again, with apologies. He'd tried everything to get out of a sudden meeting but it was impossible. Would Joanna mind having dinner without him?

She bit her lip to keep from saying that she'd already had dinner without him last night; what would be the difficulty in doing it again?

"Of course not," she said briskly. "We'll have dessert and coffee together, when you get home."

But he didn't get home until almost ten, and by then she was in bed.

She heard his footsteps first on the stairs, then coming down the hall. They stopped just outside her closed door and her heart stopped, too.

Joanna held her breath, imagining her husband's hand on the knob, imagining the door slowly opening...

The footsteps moved on. Further down the hall, a door

opened, then softly shut and she fell back against the pillows in relief.

It *was* relief she felt, wasn't it?

Of course it was. What else could it be?

He was waiting for her in the dining room when she came down the next morning.

"Good morning," he said. "Sorry about last night."

"No problem," she said with a shrug of her shoulders. "I needed an early night anyway. I'm not operating on all burners yet."

David nodded. His hair was damp, as if he'd just finished showering, and suddenly she remembered what he'd said about running in the park early each morning.

"Were you out running?"

"Yes. I didn't wake you, did I? Going out so early, I mean."

"No, no, I slept like a log. I was only going to say..."

"What?"

What, indeed? They'd already talked about running together and he'd made it crystal clear that he hadn't wanted her company in the past. Why on earth would he want it now?

"I was only going to say that...that I'll have to get out for a walk, considering we're so near the park."

"Next week."

"What?"

"I said—"

"I heard what you said, David, I just didn't believe it. Or am I in the habit of asking your permission before I do something?"

His mouth twisted. "I only meant that you should wait until you're stronger."

"I am not ill," she said, her eyes flashing. "I've told you, I'm not—"

"An invalid. Yes, so you have. But going out alone, in a neighborhood that's strange to you, might be daunting."

She smiled through stiff lips. "New York still has street

signs, doesn't it? Believe me, I'll find my way home without sprinkling bread crumbs behind me."

To her surprise, he laughed. "I'll bet you will." His smile faded. They stood looking at each other in an increasingly uncomfortable silence and then he cleared his throat. "Well, it's getting late. You'll forgive me if I hurry off, Jo, won't you?"

"Of course."

She smiled brightly as he picked up a leather briefcase from a table near the door. After a barely perceptible hesitation, he bent and dropped a light kiss on her forehead.

"Have a good day," he said. And he was gone.

A good day, Joanna thought. Tears stung her eyes.

"Mrs. Adams?"

Joanna blinked hard, took a steadying breath and turned around to see the housekeeper standing in the doorway to the dining room.

"Yes, Mrs. Timmons?"

"Your breakfast is ready. Half a grapefruit and black coffee, as usual."

"Oh. Thank you. I'll be... Mrs. Timmons?"

"Madam?"

"Was that my usual? My breakfast, I mean. Grapefruit and black coffee?"

The housekeeper's lips thinned in disapproval. "For as long as it mattered, it was."

"Do you think we might try something different?"

Mrs. Timmons's brows lifted a little. "We could, if you wish. What would you like?"

Joanna blushed. "I don't really know. I mean...I'm open to suggestion."

"Cinnamon toast," the housekeeper said, her eyes on Joanna's face, "orange juice, and hot chocolate."

"Hot chocolate!" Joanna laughed. "No, I don't think so."

"Coffee, then, but with sugar and cream. How does that sound, madam?"

"It sounds lovely." Joanna took a breath. "Do you have a minute to talk, Mrs. Timmons?"

The housekeeper's eyes narrowed. "If you wish."

Joanna ran the tip of her tongue over her lips. "Well, to begin with, I'd be pleased if you called me 'Joanna.'"

Mrs. Timmons's face paled. "I couldn't possibly do that, madam."

"Then call me 'Mrs. Adams.' Just don't...don't keep calling me 'madam.'" Joanna gave a little laugh. "I have enough trouble thinking of myself as 'Joanna,' let alone as anybody called 'madam.'"

The older woman's mouth opened, then shut again. After a moment, she nodded.

"I'll try and remember that, ma...Mrs. Adams."

"And I was wondering... Do you know who...uh, who furnished this house?"

"Why, you did, of course."

Joanna sighed. The answer was unpleasant, but not exactly a surprise.

"There's just one last thing..." She hesitated. "What did I usually do with my days?"

"Breakfast at eight, your health club at ten, and then, of course, your afternoons were quite full."

"Full? Do you mean...do I have some kind of part-time job?"

Joanna had the uneasy feeling that it was all Mrs. Timmons could do to keep from laughing.

"Certainly not, Mrs. Adams. You had your lunches, your charity commitments, your board meetings."

"Oh. I see."

"And then there were your three times a week hairdresser's appointments—"

"I had my hair done three times a week?" Joanna said, her voice rising in disbelief.

"You have a standing appointment on Friday at the nail salon, and, of course, there are your massages..."

"My massages," Joanna echoed faintly. She wanted to laugh. Or maybe she wanted to cry. It was hard to know which.

"You might wish to check your appointment book. Perhaps it's in the library. Or in your desk, in your bedroom."

"That's all right," Joanna said quickly, "I'll, ah, I'll forego all that for a while, until I'm feeling more like my old self…"

Her old self, who was beginning to sound more and more like one absolutely, monumentally pretentious bore.

The day was a duplicate of the one before.

She wandered through the house. She read. She sat in the garden. She had lunch, took a nap, and woke as restless as a tiger.

In midafternoon, she took a light jacket and headed for the door. Hollister, appearing from out of nowhere, reached it the same instant.

"If madam wishes to go anywhere," he said, "I am at her disposal."

"Thank you," Joanna said politely, "but I'm going for a walk."

"A walk, madam?"

"Yes," she said. "You know, left foot, right foot…a walk. In the park."

"Madam might wish to reconsider…"

Joanna yanked open the door. "Madam is out of here," she said, and slammed the door behind her.

The walk cleared her head.

She'd snapped at David this morning, and then at Hollister. There was no reason for it; everyone meant well, and she knew it.

It was she who was being difficult, not the staff or her husband.

It was just that it all seemed so strange…a wry smile curved over her lips as she made her way up the stairs to her room. This was the life she'd led, but was this the life she'd wanted?

It didn't seem possible.

Ellen was in the bathroom, pouring perfumed oil into the tub.

"There you are, ma'am. I'm just running your bath."

Joanna sighed and sat down on the edge of the bed.

"Ellen, do you think you could stop calling me 'ma'am'? I keep expecting to turn around and find the Queen of England hovering just over my shoulder."

Ellen giggled. "As you wish, madam."

"What I wish," Joanna said, "is that you'd call me Mrs. Adams."

"Oh, but, madam… You were very specific when you hired me, you said I was to address you as 'ma'am' or 'madam.'"

"Just forget whatever I said," Joanna said, more sharply than she'd intended. "I mean…things have changed. Besides, if you call me 'Mrs. Adams' it will help me get used to the sound of my own name."

"Yes, Mrs. Adams."

Joanna smiled. "Thank you. Now, what's this about running a bath?"

"Well, you bathe every day at this time, ma…Mrs. Adams. Then you dress for dinner."

"Dress?" Joanna looked down at herself. She was wearing a navy dress and matching kidskin pumps. Dreary, she thought, and frowned.

"Yes, Mrs. Adams."

"As in, long gown, white gloves and tiara?"

"Not quite so formal," Ellen said seriously. "A short dress, no gloves, and I suppose I could find a comb for your chignon, if you like."

"Do I do this every night? Dress for dinner, I mean?"

"Oh, yes, Mrs. Adams, you do."

Joanna's smile faded. A morning spent doing a lot of nothing, then an afternoon doing more of the same, followed by a soak in a perfumed bath while she considered what dress to wear for dinner.

What a useless existence.

Was this what it meant to be David Adams's wife? She thought of how he'd looked on Sunday, when he'd taken her away from Bright Meadows. The faded jeans, so worn and snug they'd outlined his body, the sweatshirt, straining over

his broad shoulders. She thought of his admission that he
never let anyone work on his car except him.

Why would a man like that marry a woman who made an
art of doing nothing?

"My—my husband dresses for dinner, too?"

"Oh, yes. Mr. Adams showers and changes to a dark suit."
Ellen sighed. "I think it's just so old-fashioned and romantic."

Old-fashioned. Romantic. Joanna's pulse quickened. Perhaps she was getting the wrong picture. Dressing for dinner
didn't have to be stuffy, it could be everything Ellen had just
called it.

"All right," she said, "I'll tell you what. I'll shower, and
you pick a dress for me to wear tonight."

"Shower? But—"

"Trust me, Ellen. Unless I'm shivering cold or dying of the
flu, I'm not a bath person."

The maid looked at her, her face puzzled. Two out of two,
Joanna thought, remembering the way Mrs. Timmons had
looked at her this morning. Neither her maid nor her housekeeper could fit the present Joanna Adams inside the skin of
the old, and if you added Joanna Adams herself, the score
went to a perfect three out of three.

It was a sobering, even frightening, thought.

At seven, dressed in black *peau de soie*, Joanna started down
the stairs.

The dress wasn't much to her liking—it was blousey, almost
shapeless, not short enough to be sexy or long enough to be
fashionable, and it made her feel twice her age. But then, that
description pretty much fit everything in her closet.

Why on earth had she bought all that clothing?

She'd as much as asked the question of Ellen, who'd
shrugged.

"You shopped at all the best stores, Mrs. Adams."

"Did I?" Joanna had said softly, staring into the mirror.

Maybe she'd forgotten more than the details of her own life,
she thought as she reached the bottom of the staircase; maybe
she'd forgotten the tenets of high fashion.

She hung on to that thought as she paused in the doorway to the library. She could see David waiting for her before the fireplace, his back to her, one foot up on the edge of the stone hearth, his hands tucked into the pockets of his trousers.

What a handsome man he was, even from this angle. Those incredible shoulders. Those long legs and that tight bottom...

Her taste in furniture, clothes and hairstyles might be in doubt. But her taste in men seemed to have been impeccable.

David turned around.

"Joanna," he said.

Color flew into her cheeks.

"David." She swallowed dryly. "Hello."

His gaze swept over her. She waited for him to say something complimentary about her appearance but he didn't. She studied his face, trying to read his expression, but it was like trying to read the face of a statue.

"Well," she said brightly, "how was your day?"

"It was fine," he said evenly. "How was yours?"

Her heart sank. They were going to have another one of their standard, oh-so-polite conversations. How was your day? he'd asked and she was supposed to say it was fine, it was pleasant, it was...

"Dull."

David's eyebrows lifted. "Dull?"

"Well, yes. I didn't do anything."

His eyes narrowed. "You did something. You went for a walk."

Her head came up. "Ah, I see Hollister reported in, did he?"

"Hollister was only following orders."

"You mean, you told him to spy on me?"

David ran his hand through his hair. "It's been a long day, Jo. Let's not quarrel."

"Do we?" Joanna said quickly. "Quarrel, I mean?"

"No," he said, after a pause, "not really." It was true. Even their decision to divorce had been reached in a civilized way. No raised voices, no anger...no regrets. "Why do you ask?"

Because at least, if we quarreled, there was something more than this terrible nothingness between us…

She sighed. "No reason. I just wondered."

"Look, I'm only trying to make sure you don't overdo."

She sighed again. "I know."

"Before you know it, you'll be phoning up old friends, going to lunch, maybe even attending one or two of those meetings of yours."

"Yuck."

"Yuck?" David laughed. "Did you say 'yuck'?"

She blushed. "I meant to say that, uh, that doesn't sound very exciting, either."

Why had she let the conversation take this turn? David was watching her with a sudden intensity that made her feel like a mouse under the eye of a hungry cat. There was no way she could explain what she felt to him when she couldn't even explain it to herself.

"Don't pay any attention to me," she said with a little laugh. "I've probably been lying around feeling sorry for myself for too long." She turned away from him, searching desperately for a diversion. Her gaze fell on the built-in bar across the room. "What great-looking hors d'oeuvres," she said, hurrying toward them. "Cheese, and olives…what's this?"

"*Chèvre*," David said as she picked up a tiny cracker spread with a grainy white substance and popped it into her mouth.

"*Chèvre*?"

"Goat cheese."

Joanna stared at him. "Goat cheese?" Her nose wrinkled.

"Yeah. You love the stuff."

She shuddered, snatched up a cocktail napkin, and wiped her mouth.

"Not anymore."

He grinned. "It's even worse than it sounds. That's not just goat cheese, it's goat cheese rolled in ash."

"Ash?" she repeated in amazement. "As in, what's on the end of a cigarette?"

His grin widened. "I don't think so, but does it really matter?"

"You're right, it doesn't. Ash. And goat cheese." She laughed. "What will they think of next?"

"Chocolate-dipped tofu," he said solemnly. Her eyes widened and he held up his hand. "Scout's honor. It was part of the buffet at a business dinner last week. The Halloran merger. You remem... A deal I've been working on."

Her smile slipped, but only a little. "And how was the chocolate-dipped tofu?"

"I didn't touch the stuff. Morgana tried it and said it was great, but you know..." He frowned. "Sorry, Jo. I keep forgetting. Morgana is my P.A."

"Your...?"

"Personal Assistant."

Joanna nodded. "Oh. And she—she went to this dinner with you?"

"Of course." He hesitated. "She'd like to stop by and see you. She's wanted to, ever since the accident, but I told her I wasn't sure if you were up to seeing visitors, even when they're old friends."

Old friends? A woman named Morgana, who spent more time with her husband than she did? His assistant? His personal assistant?

"That was thoughtful of you, David. Please tell—Morgana—that I need just a little more time, would you?"

"Of course."

Joanna smiled at him, her lips curving up softly, and he realized that she'd inadvertently wiped away all that bright red lipstick she favored and he despised. Her mouth was full, pink and softly inviting, and he suddenly wondered what she'd do if leaned down and kissed it. He wouldn't touch her; he'd just kiss her, stroke the tip of his tongue across that sweet, lush flesh...

Hell!

"Well," he said briskly, "how about a drink?"

He didn't wait for an answer. Instead, he poured some bourbon for himself and sherry for Joanna. Her fingers closed around the delicate stem of the glass as he handed it to her.

"To your recovery," he said, raising his glass.

She echoed the sentiment, then took a sip of her drink. The pale gold liquid slipped down her throat and she grimaced.

"What's wrong?" David said. "Has the sherry gone bad?"

"It's probably just me. This is just a little bit dry for my taste, that's all."

He looked at her. "Is it?"

"But it's good," she said quickly. "Really."

"Come on, Jo. I can see that you don't like it."

She hesitated. "But...but I used to," she said in a suddenly small voice, "didn't I?"

"Tastes change," he said with studied casualness. "I'll pour you something else. What would you prefer?"

A picture popped instantly into her head. A bottle, dark amber in color, with a red and white label...

"Jo?"

She smiled uneasily. "I know this is going to sound ridiculous, but...I just thought of something called Pete's Wicked Ale."

David went very still. "Did you?"

"Isn't that crazy? Who'd name something... What's the matter?"

"You used to drink Pete's." His voice was low, almost a whisper. "A long time ago, before you decided that sherry was...that you preferred sherry to ale."

Joanna began to tremble. "Oh, God!"

"Easy." David took the glass from her hand. He led her to the sofa and helped her sit. "Put your head down and take a deep breath."

"I'm...I'm OK."

"You're not OK, you're as white as a sheet."

"I just...what's happening to me, David?" She lifted her face to his and stared at him through eyes that had gone from violet to black.

"You're remembering things, that's all."

"It's more than that." Her voice shook. "I feel as if I'm

trapped inside a black tunnel and—and every now and then I look up and I see a flash of light, but it never lasts long enough for me to really see anything.''

"Dammit, Joanna, put your head down!'' David put his hand on her hair and forced her face toward her knees. "I knew this would happen if you went sailing off as if nothing had happened to you.''

"I'm not sick!'' She shoved at his hand and leaped to her feet. "Didn't you listen to anything I said? I'm—I'm lost, David, lost, and I can't...I can't...''

Her eyes rolled up into her head and she began to slump to the floor. David cursed, caught her in his arms, and strode from the dining room.

"Ellen,'' he bellowed. "Mrs. Timmons!''

The housekeeper and the maid came running. When Mrs. Timmons saw David hurrying up the stairs with Joanna in his arms, her hands flew to her mouth.

"Oh, my Lord, Mr. David, what happened?''

"Ellen, you get some ice. Mrs. Timmons, you call the doctor. Tell him my wife's fainted and I want him here now.''

"Yes, sir. I'll do my best but it's after hours and—''

"Just get him, dammit!'' David shouldered open the door to Joanna's room. Her eyes fluttered open as he lay her down gently on the bed.

"David?'' she whispered. "What...what happened?''

"You're all right,'' he said gently. "You fainted, that's all.''

"Fainted.'' She made a sound he supposed was a laugh. God, her face was as pale as the pillow sham. "I couldn't have fainted. It's—it's so Victorian.''

"Sir?'' David looked around. Ellen was standing in the doorway, her eyes wide, with a basin of ice and a towel.

"That's fine, Ellen. Just bring that to me—thank you. And shut the door after you when you leave.''

Joanna stared up at him, her face still pale. "I can't believe I fainted.''

"Well, you did. You overdid,'' he said grimly. "Too much,

too soon, that's all. Can you turn your head a bit? That's the way.''

"My head hurts," she said, and winced. "What are you doing?"

"What does it look like I'm doing? I'm getting you out of this dress."

She caught his hand but he shrugged her off and went on opening the tiny jet buttons that ran down the front of the black silk dress.

"David, don't. I'm OK. I can—"

"You can't," he said, even more grimly, "and you won't. Dammit, woman, how can a dress be tight enough at the throat to cut off your air and so loose everyplace else that it turns you into a sack of potatoes?"

"A sack of…" Joanna flushed. "You don't like this dress?"

"I don't like flour sacks. What man does? And what the hell does what I like or not like have to do with what you wear? Sit up a little. That's it. Now lift your arm…the other one. Good girl."

She stared at him as he tossed the dress aside. "But I thought…I assumed…" She thought of the closetful of ugly clothes, of the awful furniture in the room, of the servants David had so pointedly said were hers, and her mouth began to tremble.

"I don't understand," she whispered.

"Turn on your side."

She obeyed without thinking. His voice was toneless, his touch as impersonal as a physician's. She felt his hands at the nape of her neck, and then her hair came tumbling down over her shoulders.

"There," he said, "that's better. No wonder your head hurts. You've got enough pins stuck into your scalp to…to…"

His angry, rushed words ground to a halt. He had turned her toward him again and as he looked down at her, his heart seemed to constrict within his chest.

She was so beautiful. So much the woman he still remembered, the woman he'd never been able to get out of his mind.

Stripped of the ugly dress, her hair flowing down over her creamy shoulders, her eyes wide and fixed on his, she was everything he remembered, everything he'd ever wanted, and the name he'd once called her whispered from his lips.

"Gypsy," he said huskily.

Who? Joanna thought, who? It wasn't her name, surely... and yet, as she looked up in David's eyes and saw the way he was looking at her, she felt as if she were falling back to another time and place.

Gypsy, she thought, oh, yes, she would be his Gypsy, if that was what he wanted, she would dance for him by firelight, she would whirl around him in an ever-tightening circle until she fell into his waiting arms. She would do whatever he asked of her, she would love him forever...

"Joanna," he whispered.

He bent toward her, then hesitated. Joanna didn't think, she simply reached up, clasped his face and brought him to her.

His mouth closed over hers.

His kiss was gentle, soft and sweet. But she could feel him trembling and she knew what was happening, that he was fighting to control what was raging through him, the need to plunder her mouth, to ravage her until she cried out with need. She knew, because it was raging through her, too.

"David," she sighed.

He groaned and his arms swept around her as he came down on the bed beside her. Her body was soft as silk and hot as the sun against his; his hand swept up and cupped her breast; she moaned and he felt her nipple spring to life beneath the silk of her slip and press against his palm...

"Mr. Adams?"

He raised his head and stared blindly at the closed door. Someone was knocking on it and calling his name.

"Mr. Adams? It's Ellen, sir. Dr. Corbett's arrived. Shall I send him up?"

David looked down at Joanna. Her face was flushed with color, her eyes were dark as the night. Her mouth was softly swollen and pink from his kisses....

But it meant nothing. Nothing. If he valued his own sanity, he had to keep remembering that.

His wife, his beautiful, lying wife, was unexcelled at this game. Her body still remembered how to play, even if her mind did not.

"David?"

Her voice was as soft as it always was. It was her heart that was hard.

"David," she said again, and he stood up, took her robe from where it lay at the foot of the bed, and tossed it to her.

"Cover yourself," he said coldly, and then he turned his back on his wife and on temptation.

CHAPTER SIX

JOANNA was stunned by the tone of cold command in her husband's voice.

"What?"

"You heard me," he growled. "Cover yourself—unless you don't object to Corbett knowing what you were up to a minute ago."

She felt the blood drain from her face. "What *I* was up to?"

"All right. What we were up to. Does that make you feel better?"

She grabbed the robe he'd tossed to her and shoved her arms through the sleeves. She was trembling, not with the aftermath of desire but with the fury of humiliation.

"Nothing could make me feel better," she said shakily, "except being able to start my life beginning the day before I met you."

"My sentiments exactly. The sooner you get your memory back, the better it will be for the both of us."

Joanna swung her legs to the floor and stood up, stumbling a little as she did. David reached out to help her but she swatted his hands away.

"Don't touch me. Don't you ever touch me again. Do you understand?"

David stared at his wife. Her eyes blazed black in her face. Suddenly, he was overcome with guilt. What had just happened was as much his fault as hers. Hell, who was he kidding? It was all his fault. She had no memory but he—he remembered everything. And she was right. She hadn't started this ugly scene, he had.

"Joanna," he said, "listen—"

"Get out of my room."

"Jo, please, I'm trying to apolo—"

She snatched a perfume bottle from the vanity and hurled it at him. He ducked and it whizzed by his head and shattered against the wall just as the door banged open.

Doctor Corbett paused in the doorway. He looked at the shards of glass that glittered against the carpet, then cleared his throat and raised a politely inquisitive face to David and Joanna.

"Excuse me," he said, "is there a problem here?"

"Yes!" Joanna glared at David. "I want this man out of my room!"

Corbett turned to David. "Mr. Adams," he said gently, "perhaps you'll give me a few moments alone with your..."

"Be my guest, Doctor. Take a few years, if you like," David snarled.

The door slammed shut after him. The doctor waited and then cleared his throat again.

"Well, Mrs. Adams," he said briskly, "why don't you tell me what's going on here?"

Joanna swung toward him. "I'll tell you what's going on," she said furiously. "I'll tell you what's...what's..." Her shoulders slumped. She felt the rage that had been driving her draining from her system. "Oh, hell," she muttered, "hell!" She sank down on the edge of her bed and wiped her sleeve across suddenly damp eyes. "I want my memory back," she said in a choked whisper. "Is that asking so much?"

"My dear Mrs. Adams—"

"Don't call me that!" Joanna's head snapped up, her eyes gleaming once again with anger. "It's bad enough I'm married to that—that cold-blooded Neanderthal! I certainly don't need to be reminded of it all the time."

Corbett sighed. Then he pulled a Kleenex from a box on the table beside Joanna's bed and handed it to her.

"Suppose you tell me what happened tonight," he said quietly. "All I really know is that your housekeeper phoned my service and said you'd collapsed."

"I didn't collapse!" Joanna dabbed at her eyes, wiped her nose, then balled up the tissue and threw it into a wicker wastebasket. "David blew what happened out of all proportion. I just felt woozy for a minute, that's all."

"Woozy," Corbett repeated.

"Yes. I know it's not the sort of fancy medical term you use, but…" She stopped, bit her lip, and looked at him. "I'm sorry, Doctor. I don't know why I'm letting my anger out on you."

"That's all right."

"No, it isn't. It's myself I'm angry at."

"For what?"

"What do you mean, for what?" She threw her arms wide. "For everything! For having something as stupid as amnesia, that's for what!"

"There's nothing 'stupid' about amnesia," Corbett said gently. "And you didn't have a choice in acquiring it. You suffered a head injury, and it's going to take time to heal."

"It will heal though, won't it? You said—"

"There are no guarantees but, as I've told you, I've every reason to believe your memory will return." Corbett drew out the bench from the vanity table and sat down facing her. "Right now, I'm more concerned about what you call this 'wooziness' you felt tonight. Did it come on suddenly? Or was it precipitated by some event?"

She sighed. "It didn't happen out of the blue, if that's what you're asking. I…I remembered something. Not much, there was just a momentary flash…but it startled me."

"So, it was the shock of remembering that made you feel…what? Dizzy? Weak?"

She nodded. "Yes."

"And then?" Corbett prompted.

"And then, David told Mrs. Timmons to phone you and he brought me up here and…and…" Her voice trailed off.

"And you quarreled?"

She thought of how David had undressed her, of how he'd let down her hair. Of how he'd kissed her and how she'd responded with heated, almost unbearable passion…and of how he'd reacted then, with an anger that had bordered on disgust.

"Joanna?"

Color washed over her skin. "You could say that," she murmured, and looked down at her lap.

Corbett reached for his leather medical bag. "Very well. Let's just check a few things, shall we?"

"Check whatever you like. There's nothing wrong with me. Not physically, anyway."

She was right. The doctor's examination was thorough and when it was over, he pronounced her in excellent health.

"In excellent health," Joanna said with a bitter smile. "It's like that awful old joke, the one about the operation being a success but the patient dying."

"You're making fine progress. You've started to remember things."

"A picture of a bottle of beer flashing through my head isn't exactly the same as getting my memory back, Doctor."

"Joanna." Corbett took her hand in his. "You must have patience. I know this is difficult for you and for your husband, but—"

"Oh, please!" Joanna snatched back her hand. "Don't waste your sympathy on David!"

"Surely, you realize your condition is affecting him as well as you?"

"Look," she said, after a brief hesitation, "I know I must sound like a shrew. But you can't imagine what David's like."

"No," Corbett said mildly, "I can't. I only know what I've observed, that he came to the hospital every evening of your stay, that he agreed to bring you home when you seemed unhappy at Bright Meadows, that he's stood by you during a most difficult period."

Joanna stared at the doctor. Then she gave a deep, deep sigh.

"You're right, I suppose. And I have tried to keep in mind that this can't be easy for him."

"Joanna, the worst thing about loss of memory is the pressure it brings to bear on a relationship. That's why you both need to be patient as you restructure yours.''

"Yes, but..." She hesitated. "But it's hard," she said softly, "when you don't know what things were like between you in the first place. I mean, what if...what if things had been shaky for a couple—a hypothetical couple—in the past? How could they possibly restructure a relationship successfully? One of them would know the truth and the other—the other would be working in the dark."

Corbett smiled. "There are those who would say the one working in the dark was fortunate."

"Fortunate?" Joanna's head came up. "That I don't know—that this hypothetical person doesn't know what sort of marriage she had?"

"Without a past, there can be no regrets. No anger, no recriminations... It's like starting over again with a clean slate."

Joanna laughed softly. "I didn't know they taught Optimism in med school."

"Philosophy was my love before I decided on medicine." Corbett chuckled. "Sometimes, it still comes in handy." He patted her hand, then stood up. "I'm going to give you something to help you sleep. And I'm going to leave you a prescription you must promise to follow."

"What kind of prescription? You said I was healthy."

"I want you to stop worrying about the past. *Carpe diem*, Joanna. Seize the day. The past is lost to *all* of us, not just to you. It's today and tomorrow that matter."

A slight smile curved across Joanna's lips. "More leftover class notes from Philosophy, Doctor?"

"Just an old-fashioned mother who loved quoting the classics." Corbett took a vial of tablets from his bag, shook two into her palm and poured her a glass of water from the thermos jug on the night table. "It's time you started living your life again."

"That sounds terrific, Doctor Corbett, but I don't know what 'my life' is."

"Then find out," he said briskly, snapping shut his bag.

"Surely you had friends, interests, things you enjoyed doing...?"

"From what I can gather, I seem to have made an art of doing as little as possible," she said with a faintly bitter smile.

"Then try something new. Something you can share with David, perhaps. But don't go on moping and feeling sorry for yourself."

"Me?" Joanna handed him the glass. Her voice rose in indignation. "But I haven't..." Her gaze met Corbett's. She laughed and fell back against the pillows. "That's some combination," she said wryly, "philosophy and medicine."

Corbett grinned. "Just think of me as Ann Landers, M.D." He waved a hand in salute and shut the bedroom door.

The doctor's advice made sense.

She couldn't recall the past. Much as it upset Joanna to admit it, she didn't even have any guarantee that she ever would.

So whatever condition her marriage had been in didn't matter. It was what she made of it now that counted.

David didn't seem to like her very much. Well, she thought early the next morning as she pulled on a pair of cotton shorts and a tank top, maybe she hadn't been a very likeable person.

No. That couldn't be, she thought with a smile...

But it was possible, wasn't it?

Or maybe they'd hit a rough patch in their marriage. Maybe they'd begun to drift apart.

Not that it mattered. The doctor was right. *Carpe diem.* The past was gone and only the present mattered, and when you came down to it, she didn't know all that much about the present, either, especially as it related to her husband.

Share something with David, Corbett had advised.

But what? What did her husband do with his spare time? What were his interests? Who were his friends?

Joanna glanced at her watch as she pulled her hair back into a ponytail and secured it with a coated rubber band. She had lots of questions and hardly any answers. Well, starting today, she was going to go after those answers.

Quietly, she opened the door to her bedroom and stepped out into the corridor.

David was in for a surprise.

"Surprise" wasn't the right word.

"Shocked" came closer to the truth, judging by the look on his face when he came trotting down the steps ten minutes later and saw her.

"Joanna?" He stared at her as if she might be an hallucination. "What are you doing up at this hour?"

She smiled at him over her shoulder. She'd been doing stretching exercises while she waited, using one of the marquetry benches that flanked the foyer door for support.

"Good morning," she said, as she finished her last stretch. "And it's not really so early, is it?"

He tore his astonished gaze from her and glanced at his watch.

"Are you kidding? It's just after six."

"Well, I was awake so I figured, instead of just lying in bed vegetating, I might as well get up and do something useful." She jerked her head in the direction of the kitchen. "I made a pot of coffee."

"Yes. Yes, I thought I smelled coffee."

"Would you like some?"

"No. Ah, no, thank you." He edged past her, as if she might vaporize if touched. "I prefer to wait until after my run but you go ahead and, ah, and have a cup."

"I already did." She followed after him, to the front door. "You don't mind, do you?"

"That you made coffee? No, of course not."

"That I've decided to run with you."

He swung toward her. "That you've...?" His gaze flew over her again, taking in her gray sweat shorts, her tank top, her ponytail, her running shoes. She'd decided to run with him? His brain couldn't seem to process the information. She hadn't run with him in months. In years. She hadn't done any of this in years, gotten up at this hour, put up the morning coffee, worn this tattered outfit that had once made his pulse beat quicken…hell, that *still* made his pulse beat quicken because she was the only woman he'd ever known who could fill out a shirt that way, or pair of shorts, the only one whose early morning, unmade-up face was a face that would have put Helen of Troy to shame…

Dammit, Adams, are you nuts?

"David? Do you mind?"

He frowned, shook his head. "No," he said coldly, "I suppose not."

She smiled. "Thanks. I was hoping you wouldn't mi—"

"It's a free country," he said as he swung the door open and started down toward the street. "And a big park. Just do your best to keep up, Joanna, because I don't feel much like tailoring my pace to suit yours."

Gracious. That was the word to describe her husband's acceptance of her presence, Joanna thought sarcastically as she panted after him half an hour later, gracious and charming and oh-so-welcoming.

But she was matching the pace he'd set, even if her legs were screaming and her breath was wheezing in lungs that felt as if they were on fire.

It had occurred to her, one or two times, that David was deliberately trying to exhaust her but why would he do that?

No. She was just out of shape, that was all.

But she'd be damned if she'd admit it.

Stupid. That was the word to describe his acceptance of his wife's presence, David thought grimly as he pounded through the park, stupid and pointless and all-around dumb.

Why hadn't he just told her he didn't want any part of her? That he was perfectly happy with the way things had been for the past few years, thank you very much, with him running alone and her doing her la-di-da exercises at her fancy health club.

She'd caught him off guard, that was why. Well, it wouldn't happen again. He couldn't imagine what insanity had gotten into her today, especially after what had happened between them last night. Corbett had come down from her bedroom looking smug and mysterious; he'd said she was in excellent health and that he'd advised her to get on with the business of living.

Was this Joanna's idea of how to do that?

David didn't think so. The real Joanna hadn't thought so, either, and if he was playing his cards right, this new one would soon come to the same conclusion.

He was running harder and faster than he'd run in years, running in a way that would exhaust anybody, especially a devotee of glitter Spandex, odor-free sweat and fancy treadmills.

By the time they got back to the house, she'd be finished with early morning runs and whatever foolishness had sent her along on this one.

Still, he had to admit, she was keeping up.

He frowned, put his head down, and ran harder.

But she wasn't finished with early morning runs, not by a long shot.

She was waiting for him the next morning, and the morning after that. By the third day, he adjusted his pace back to where it had been before Joanna had intruded.

He did it for her sake. Hell, it wasn't fair to tax her so, even if Corbett said she was fine.

He certainly didn't do it for his. And he certainly didn't enjoy having her tag along.

But when she wasn't bent over the bench in the foyer Friday morning, doing those stretching exercises that tilted her sexy little bottom into the air, David paused on the steps while he tried to figure out what the strange emotion stealing over him might be.

Disappointment?

No. Hell, no, why would he—

"Hi."

Joanna was standing in the door to the library, clutching a cup of coffee in her hands, smiling at him over the rim.

His heart did something absolutely stupid, as if it were on a string, yo-yoing in his chest.

"Hi," he said, and managed not to smile back.

"You're early."

"Am I? Well, that's OK, if you're not ready to—"

"I'm ready. Just let me put this cup in the sink and I'll be—"

"Jo?" He shoved his hand into his hair and scraped it back from his forehead.

"Yes?"

"I was going to say...I was going to say..."

He knew what he'd been going to say, that they might skip this morning's run, take their coffee out into the little garden, drink it together at the minuscule wrought-iron table under the tree and talk about nothing in particular and everything under the sun, just the way they used to, a million years ago.

"Yes, David?"

He looked at her. Was he crazy? He had to be. It was bad enough they'd started running together but they'd also started spending the evening together, too. Joanna waited for him to get home, no matter how late, before sitting down to dinner. He'd even begun to look forward to it, just sharing their mealtime, talking, telling her about the inconsequential bits and pieces of his day...

Why was he letting these things happen? Nothing, *nothing*, had changed. Joanna had lost her memory but sooner or later she'd get it back. She'd remember who she was and what she wanted. She'd turn into the real Joanna Adams again, the one that lay hidden beneath that mask of sexy innocence, and when she did...when she did, he had no intention of watching it happen again.

Feeling disappointment turn to despair once in a lifetime was more than enough.

He stood straighter and, with a cool smile, pulled the door open.

"I'd rather not wait, if it's all the same to you," he said politely. "I'd prefer running by myself today." The sudden hurt in her eyes knotted in his gut and his irritation with himself only made him twist the knot tighter. "Oh, by the way, Joanna…don't expect me for dinner tonight. There's a fund-raiser at the Gallery of Alternative Arts and I've agreed to attend."

Joanna stared at her husband. It had taken him no time at all to undo the progress of the past days. She wanted to weep; she wanted to slug him. Instead, she did the only thing she knew she ought to do, which was to smile brightly.

"How nice for you," she said.

"Yes, isn't it?" he answered, blithely ignoring the fact that tonight's event was just the kind of thing he hated, a bunch of fat cats standing around stroking each other's fur, telling themselves they were helping the world when all they were really doing was making asses of themselves. He hadn't even intended to go to the damned gala until desperation had forced his hand a couple of seconds ago. "Morgana reminded me of it yesterday."

"Morgana," Joanna repeated, even more brightly.

"My Personal—"

"—Assistant." She nodded. "Yes, I know."

"Anyhow, don't wait up. These things usually run late."

"Oh, of course. Well, have a good run. And a good day. And a good…"

He was gone.

Joanna stood in the open doorway, watching her husband. His stride was long and loose as he ran toward Fifth Avenue without so much as a backward glance.

Her bottom lip trembled.

So much for sharing.

So much for getting back into life.

So much for letting herself think there might be a human being lurking inside the man she was married to.

She slammed the door, made her way back to the kitchen, rinsed out her cup and put it away.

"*Carpe diem*, my foot," she muttered.

Dr. Corbett's advice had been useless. Useless. She'd wasted her time, wasted her hopes.

That's right, Joanna. You might as well go back to sitting around and feeling sorry for yourself.

Her head jerked up.

"I'm not feeling sorry for myself!"

Sure you are. You're thinking that he could have waited while you rinsed your coffee cup, that he could have asked you to go with him tonight.

Unless, of course, he was taking the ever-present, ever-helpful Morgana.

A muscle ticked in Joanna's cheek. She put her cup down, trotted up the stairs to her room and to the Queen Anne secretary that stood on one wall. There was a white-leather appointment book in the top drawer; she'd flipped through it a couple of times, shuddering at the stuff she saw scrawled over the weekly calendar pages, nonsense about hairdresser's appointments and dress fittings and luncheons and meetings that sounded senseless and silly...

There it was, under today's date, in her handwriting.

Eight p.m., Gal. of Alt. Arts, benefit for Tico the Chimp.

Her eyes widened. Tico the Chimp?

She closed the book, lay it aside, and stared into space. Tico the Chimp. The elusive Morgana. And David, all under one roof.

Joanna shucked off her running clothes and headed for the shower.

CHAPTER SEVEN

AMNESIA, as Joanna was quickly learning, was a strangely elective ailment.

She didn't remember any of the details of her own life. But when she thought back to what Ellen had said—that she shopped in only the best stores—a list came quickly to mind.

And though she'd apparently bought only dark, conservative clothing in those fashionable shops, surely they also carried other things. They had to sell dresses that were bright in color and didn't have sleeves to the wrist and hems to mid-calf, that didn't make a woman look as if she were...what had David said? As if she were a sack of potatoes?

There was only one way to find out.

Joanna dressed quickly, without giving much thought to her selections. What was there to think about, when all her clothing had a grim sameness? Even her underwear was dowdy and utilitarian.

She paid even less attention to her hair. She hadn't yet grasped the knack of neatly knotting it low on her neck. Ellen had been fixing it, most mornings, but today was her maid's day off and even if it hadn't been, Joanna was too impatient to wait while her curls were brushed and sprayed into submission. So she simply caught her hair in one hand, gave it a twist, then pinned it into place.

Ugh, she thought, grimacing as she caught a glimpse of herself in the mirror, she looked even more funereal than usual.

Not that it would matter, after this jaunt...

My God, Joanna, are you sure you know what you're doing?

"No," she said, into the silence, "I don't."

She thought of her husband's biting comments about her dress, about the way she wore her hair. She thought of her doctor's admonition that she give up searching for the past and instead concentrate on the present and the future.

She thought of Morgana, and tonight's party.

And then she took one last deep breath and set out to face New York.

She let Hollister drive her to the first store on her list, then told him not to wait.

It was not an order that pleased him.

"But, madam..."

"Go on, Hollister. Go to the park or something. Take your girl out for a spin." Joanna laughed at the look on his face. "You do have a girl, don't you?"

"Madam, really—"

"Hollister, really," she said gently, "I much prefer to do my shopping on my own."

Once inside the store, the giddiness that had been bubbling inside her since she'd read the entry in her appointment book was all but swept away by a sense of near panic.

The store was so big... Why had she come? Nothing about it was familiar; she had no idea where to start or even what to start looking for.

"Madam? May I help you?"

Joanna turned toward the smartly dressed young saleswoman who'd materialized at her elbow.

"Yes," she said gratefully. "I'd like to buy a dress. Something—something special, to wear to a party tonight."

The girl's eyes moved quickly and professionally over her.

"Certainly, madam," she replied, "if you'll just come with me...?"

Within moments, Joanna found herself in a sea of dresses.

"Here we are, madam. Did you have a preference as to color?"

"Does it matter?" Joanna said with a little laugh. She turned in a slow circle. "The only color I see is black."

The salesgirl smiled coolly. "Black is always fashionable, as madam can attest."

Joanna looked down at herself. She was wearing the first thing that had come to hand in her closet, a long-sleeved, long-skirted, incredibly expensive and incredibly unattractive two-piece dress and yes, indeed, it was black.

"Always," she said, and smiled politely at the salesgirl, "but not always interesting. Haven't you got other colors? Something in yellow, perhaps, or pale blue?" Her gaze lit on a mannequin in the next department. "Something like that, for instance."

"That?" the clerk said, her voice losing its cultured purr and rising in dismay. "But that dress is...it's heliotrope!"

"I'd have called it violet," Joanna said. The girl trailed behind as she walked toward the mannequin. "But perhaps you're right. It's lighter than a true violet."

"I don't think this is quite what madam is looking for," the clerk said with a quick, artificial smile. "The neckline is rather low."

"Shockingly low."

"The skirt is very short."

Joanna nodded. "It seems to be."

"This dress is definitely not madam's style."

"How do you know that, Miss..." Joanna peered at the salesgirl's identification tag. "How do you know that, Miss Simpson?"

"Why, from looking at...I mean, it's my job to listen to what a customer tells me and then determine what will best meet her needs."

"Then do it, please," Joanna said with a pleasant smile. "I've told you I need a special dress for this evening, and that I particularly like this one. Please show me to the fitting room and bring me this dress in a—what would you think? A ten?"

The baffled clerk stared at her. "I don't know, not for certain. It's difficult to assess madam's proper weight and shape in the dress she's wearing."

Joanna smiled wistfully. "So I've been told."

*   *   *

Size ten was too big.

Eight was perfect. And so was the dress, Joanna thought, staring at herself in the three-way dressing room mirror.

The color was wonderful, almost the same shade as her eyes and a perfect foil for her creamy skin and dark hair.

The neckline certainly was low and the skirt certainly was short...not that Fifth Avenue wasn't crowded with stylish women wearing their necklines just as deeply cut and the hems just as high. Still...

"Madam looks..." The salesclerk's stunned eyes met Joanna's in the mirror. "She looks beautiful!"

Joanna turned, frowned, and peered at herself over her shoulder. She had a sudden vision of David, seeing her in something so outrageous.

"I don't know," she said slowly. "Maybe you were right. This dress is—"

"Stunning," the girl said. "With your hair done differently and the right shoes..."

The women's eyes met in the mirror. Joanna could feel her courage slipping.

What are you doing, Joanna? What would David think?

There was no way of knowing. But I know what I think, she thought suddenly. I think I look—I think I look...

She reached behind her and gave the zipper a determined tug.

"I'll take it," she said, before she lost her courage completely.

The rest was easy.

The right shoes turned out to be conveniently waiting one department over, a pair of silver sandals with slender high heels and narrow straps, and there was a tiny purse on a silver shoulder chain to match. The right underthings—an ivory silk teddy with lacy garters and a pair of gossamer-sheer stockings—were just a couple of blocks away, almost calling out Joanna's name from the window of a stylish boutique.

There was only one last step to take.

Joanna stood before the mirrored door of a beauty salon.

Her appointment book had confirmed that she had standing appointments at this trendy place three times a week.

The door swung open and the scent of hair spray and expensive perfume came wafting out, born on a cloud of lushly romantic music.

Joanna squared her shoulders and marched inside.

The girl at the reception desk did a double take. "Oh, Mrs. Adams," she squealed, "how lovely to see you again. We'd heard you were in an accident!"

Joanna admitted that she had been, assured the receptionist that she was well on the road to recovery and said she was here to have her hair done.

"I know it's not my day but I was hoping you could fit me in."

The girl smiled. "Of course." She motioned to the glittering mirrors beyond them. "Arturo's just finishing up with a client so if you wouldn't mind waiting just a couple of secs...?"

Joanna followed the girl's pointing finger. Arturo confirmed he was her usual hairdresser by waving his hand and smiling. He was a gray-haired man in late middle age, as was his client whose hair was being pinned and sprayed into a style that was the duplicate of Joanna's.

"That's OK," she said quickly, "someone else can do my hair today."

"We wouldn't dream of letting that happen, Mrs. Adams. I promise, Arturo will only be—"

"How about him?"

The girl's eyes widened. The man Joanna had indicated was young, with shoulder-length hair and a tiny gold stud in one earlobe. He was cutting the hair of a woman in her midtwenties—just about my age, Joanna thought with a surprised start—and shaping it into a style that was swingy, sexy and feminine.

"Oh, but, Mrs. Adams," the receptionist said nervously, "I don't think Mick's the right guy for—"

"I think he's perfect," Joanna said, ignoring the butterflies swarming in her stomach. She smiled, sat down in an empty chair and piled her gaily wrapped packages beside her. "And

I'll be happy to wait until he's free. Oh, by the way...the sign outside says you do cosmetic makeovers, too. Is that right?"

The girl's throat worked. "Uh—uh, yes. Yes, we do. In fact, Mick is the one who—"

"Great." Joanna plucked a magazine from a lamp table, opened it and buried her face inside. After a moment, the receptionist took her cue and fled.

Joanna let out a shuddering breath and thought how perfect it would be if only the butterflies would do the same.

She taxied home, locked herself into her bedroom. Then, like a cygnet exchanging its dull feathers for the glorious plumage of a swan, she took off her old clothes and replaced them with the new.

The teddy first, and the sheer stockings followed by the violet dress, which floated down around her like the petals of a flower. She slipped on the silver shoes. Thanks to Mick, her hair was now loose on her shoulders, layered just lightly around her face. It needed only a fluff of the brush, and her new makeup—eyeliner, mascara and a touch of pale lip gloss—was easy enough to touch up, even with trembling hands.

Because her hands were trembling now, and her teeth were tapping together like castanets.

What in the hell had prompted her to do this?

She swung toward the mirrored wall against which the vanity table stood and stared at herself. She had awakened in a hospital room weeks ago, a stranger to herself.

Now, she'd replaced that stranger with another, one David had never seen before.

The enormity of what she was doing almost buckled her knees. But there was no going back now.

Joanna gave her reflection a shaky smile.

"*Carpe diem*, kid," she whispered, and gave herself a thumbs-up.

She hadn't only seized the day, she was about to wring it dry.

* * *

David was sitting behind his oak desk in his spacious office in lower Manhattan, his chair turned to the window and his back to the door, staring sightlessly over the gray waters of the Hudson River while he mentally cursed his own stupidity.

What other word could you use to describe the way he'd trapped himself into the upcoming evening of unrelieved boredom?

He'd attended parties like tonight's in the past. Joanna belonged to virtually every committee around; she'd dragged him from one mind-numbing gala to another, all in the name of what she considered to be "Good Causes," where the same dull people stood in little clusters talking about the same dull things while they chomped on soggy hors d'oeuvres and sipped flat champagne.

Finally, he'd put his foot down and said he'd write checks to Save the Somalian Snail and the Androgynous Artists of America but he'd be damned if he'd go to one more inane benefit on their behalf.

In a way, that had been the beginning of the end. He'd taken a good, hard look at the four years of his marriage and admitted the truth, that the Joanna he'd married had metamorphosed into a woman he didn't understand, a woman who was interested in knowing the right people and buying the right labels, whose only goal was to be accepted in the upper echelons of New York society...

...Who had loved his money and his position but not him. Never him.

He had to admit, she'd done a fine job of pulling the wool over his eyes. She'd been so young, so seemingly innocent, and he'd been so crazy about her that he'd even worried, at the beginning, that he might overwhelm her with the intensity of his love.

He'd admitted as much to Morgana, who knew him better than anyone after working beside him for five years, and she'd generously offered him the benefit of her insight into the members of her own sex.

"I understand, David," she'd said. "Joanna's a child, only

twenty-two to your thirty, and a free spirit, at that. You must be careful that you don't make her feel trapped.''

His mouth twisted. He needn't have worried. While he'd been busy trying to keep his wife from feeling trapped, she'd been busy rearranging his life until the night they'd been at some stupid charity ball and he'd suddenly realized that *he* was the one who was trapped, in a loveless marriage to a woman with whom he had absolutely nothing in common and never would have.

Until the accident. Until a bump on the head had wiped away Joanna's memory and turned her into...

''Dammit,'' he said.

It was dangerous to think that way. The accident hadn't ''turned'' her into anything but a woman struggling to recover her memory. Once she did, life would return to normal and so would Joanna.

And then they'd be back where they'd been a couple of months ago, with their divorce only days away, and that was just fine. It was better than fine, it was freedom. It was—

''David?''

He swung his chair around. Morgana had inched open the door to his office, just enough so she could peer around the edge.

''I'm sorry to bother you, David. I knocked, but...''

''Morgana.'' He straightened in his chair, feeling strangely guilty for having been caught with his thoughts anywhere but on the papers strewn across his desk, and smiled at his assistant. ''Come in.''

''Are you sure?'' she said, as she stepped inside the office. ''If you're busy...''

''Don't be foolish. I'm never too busy to talk to you and anyway, I really wasn't working. I was thinking about—about this party I'm supposed to go to tonight. Did you phone and say I'd changed my mind about not attending?''

''I did. And Mrs. Capshaw herself told me to assure you it wasn't too late. She wanted you to know that the entire Planning Committee would be delighted to know you'd decided to come.''

David smiled thinly. "How nice."

"She asked if Joanna would be with you." Morgana's perfect features settled into serious lines. "I told her it was far too soon for Joanna to be up and about. Which reminds me, David, I haven't asked in days...I do so want to stop by for a visit. Do you think she's up to seeing anyone yet?"

"That's kind of you, Morgana, but—"

"It isn't kind at all. I've always liked Joanna, you know that. And I know how difficult this must be for her and for you both." She hesitated, the tip of her pink tongue just moistening the fullness of her bottom lip. "She hasn't shown any signs of recovery yet, I suppose?"

The muscle in David's cheek knotted. "No."

"It will be good for her, knowing you've gone to a party she helped plan."

"She doesn't know she helped plan it."

"Oh? But I thought—I assumed that was why you decided to attend."

David frowned. Morgana was his assistant and his friend, and from the time of his marriage, she'd been Joanna's friend, too. But he wasn't about to tell her that he'd decided to go to tonight's gala only to make it clear to his wife that their lives went in separate directions...

...And what a stupid thing that had been to do, when he could make the same point just as easily and far more comfortably by going home and asking Mrs. Timmons to serve him his supper on a tray in his study.

"Actually," he said with a little smile, "now that I think about it, I'm not sure why I decided to attend. Eating soggy hors d'oeuvres and drinking flat champagne while I stare at the paintings of some artist who probably needs a bath more than he needs a paintbrush—"

"It's Tico the Chimp."

"What's Tico the Chimp?"

"The artist. You know, they profiled him in the *Times* a couple of weeks ago. The party's in his honor."

"That's just great." David began to laugh. "Soggy hors

d'oeuvres, flat champagne...and for the guest of honor, a bunch of bananas.''

''The art critic for the *Times* called him a great talent.''

''Why doesn't that surprise me? Morgana, do me a favor. Phone Mrs. Capshaw, offer my regrets—''

''The mayor's going to be there, and Senator Williamson, and the Secretary-General of the UN. I know they're all friends of yours, but—''

''Acquaintances.''

''Either way, it can't hurt to touch bases with all three of them with this new project in our laps.'' A sympathetic smile softened his assistant's patrician features. ''Besides, it will be good for you to get out a bit. I know it's not my place to say so, but these last weeks surely must have been a strain.''

David nodded. Morgana was the only person, aside from his attorney and Joanna's, who knew he and his wife had been about to divorce when the accident had occurred. Of course, she didn't know any of the details. Still, it helped that he didn't have to pretend with her.

''Yes,'' he said quietly, ''it has been.'' He drew a deep breath, then let it out slowly. ''For Joanna, too.''

''Oh, certainly.''

Morgana sat down on the edge of his desk, as she often did, and the skirt of her pale yellow suit hitched a couple of inches above her knees.

He almost smiled. When she became engrossed in something, her skirt would often hitch up, or she'd forget that her neckline might delicately gape open as she leaned forward to draw his attention to an item in her hand.

He'd have thought such things were deliberate if any other woman had done them but Morgana, though beautiful, was incapable of playing such games. She was the complete professional, a quality he'd come to appreciate more and more during the years she'd been working for him.

She'd started in his office as his secretary.

''But I don't intend to stay in that position,'' she'd told him bluntly when he'd hired her.

David had admired her drive. And the company had benefitted from it. Morgana was single-minded in her pursuit of success; she was nothing like the girls who'd preceded her, who'd batted their lashes a lot better than they took dictation or kept his files.

Not that she didn't have a heart. When he'd come to work one morning and announced he'd married the girl he'd met not ten days before, Morgana had probably been as stunned as his colleagues. But she hadn't shown it. If anything, she'd gone out of her way to befriend his young wife and ease her into his sophisticated world.

Little had he or Morgana known that Joanna had been more than ready to do that by herself.

Ever since the accident, Morgana had put her private life on hold, pitching in to take up the slack when he'd been out of the office the first couple of days, then staying late to help him play catch-up while Joanna was at Bright Meadows. He knew she was right, that there'd be networking opportunities at tonight's party...

...Opportunities she could take advantage of all on her own.

David felt a load lift from his shoulders. Why hadn't it occurred to him before? Morgana would get the chance to enjoy herself—she was far better than he at putting on a polite, social mask. And he'd be off the hook.

"You know," he said, "you could use some time off, too."

"That's kind of you to say, David, but—"

"Would you like to go to that party tonight?"

Her lovely face lit. "Why...I would, yes."

He smiled. "Well, then, why not go?"

"Oh." She gave an uncharacteristically breathless laugh. "How generous. Thank you, David. I'd enjoy that very much."

"Here," he said, opening his desk drawer and digging out his tickets for the event. "You take these and—"

"No, you'd better hang on to them." Morgana got to her feet. "I'll have to go home and change first, but I promise, I won't take very long. I can meet you at the gallery. Will that be OK?"

"Morgana," he said quickly, "you don't—"

"Oh, it's lovely of you to say that, David." She laughed again, that same soft, breathless sound. "But I can't possibly go to a party dressed like this. I promise, I'll be there by eight and not a moment later."

A dull pain began to throb behind David's eyes.

"Don't worry about it," he said wearily. "We'll take a taxi to your place. I'll wait while you change."

Morgana's smile flashed like a thousand-watt bulb.

"Oh, David, you're so kind! I just know we'll have a wonderful time."

"Yeah." He smiled, too, and the pain in his head intensified. "I just know it, too."

The hors d'oeuvres weren't soggy. They were stale.

The champagne wasn't flat. It was awful.

As for Tico the Chimp...the animal loped around the gallery, hand in hand with his owner, both of them decked out in tuxedos complete with top hats and bow ties. Every now and then, Tico rolled back his lips and let loose with a cackling shriek.

It was, David thought, the most honest comment anybody in the packed room made all night.

The whole thing was ludicrous, right down to the wild blobs of color that hung on the wall, each of them bearing the chimp's official handprint. Or was it footprint? David fought back the wild desire to ask. Everybody in the place was taking things so seriously, even Morgana.

Well, no. She couldn't be, she was too intelligent to swallow garbage like this but she was certainly putting on an amazing face, peering intently at the paintings, nodding over the notes in the program. Now, as he waited patiently, she'd lined up to shake Tico's hand. Or his paw. Or whatever in hell you called it.

It was hard to imagine Joanna as part of the committee that had planned this event even knowing, as he did, the penchant his wife had shown for fitting readily into the time-wasting habits of the idle rich. It was especially difficult because, for some crazy reason, he kept thinking back to the first one of these things they'd attended together.

They'd only been married a couple of months then and half the reason he'd decided to go to the party was because he could hardly wait to show off his gorgeous bride.

"Are we supposed to dress up?" she'd asked him and he'd kissed away the worried frown between her eyebrows and assured her that whatever she wore, she'd be the most beautiful woman in the room.

And she had been. She'd worn a hot pink dress, very demure and proper except that beneath it there'd been the hint of her lush, lovely body; her hair had streamed down over her shoulders like a midnight cloud. She'd clung to his arm, trying to look suitably impressed by—what had been on exhibit that night?

A display of cardboard boxes, that was it, some arranged on the walls, some grouped on the floor, all of them with price tags attached that made them Art instead of cardboard. They'd strolled from one end of the room to the other and then he'd bent his head to Joanna's and whispered that when they got back to Connecticut, he was going to go through the entire house, sign every box he found and then donate them all to the museum.

Joanna had looked up at him, her eyes wide and her lovely mouth trembling, and then she'd burst into laughter so hard that she'd had to bury her face against his chest.

An ache, sharper than the pain behind his eyes, crushed David's heart. Why was he thinking such dumb thoughts? That had been a million years ago. And it hadn't been real, it had all been illusion, just like Joanna herself.

If only he could forget the look of her, the sound of her voice...

"Hello, David."

The words were soft but their power stopped his breath. He turned slowly and there she was, as he remembered her. No artifice. No cool, matronly elegance. She wore little makeup, her hair was a glorious tide of midnight waves that tumbled down her back. Her dress was almost the color of her eyes; it clung to her breasts and narrow waist before flaring into a short, full skirt that stopped above her knees and made the most of her long legs.

Had he gone completely around the bend? Had he conjured up this image? For a minute he thought that maybe he had...but then she gave him a tremulous smile and he knew that she was real, this was Joanna, this was his beautiful, once-upon-a-time wife standing before him like a remembered vision come to life.

"I know I should have phoned and told you I was coming but..."

Say something, he told himself fiercely. But what?

"I hope you're not angry. It's just that I looked in my appointment book and saw that I was supposed to be here tonight and I thought, well, perhaps it's time I began to pick up the pieces of my life, and so—and so..."

Damn! Joanna bit down on her bottom lip. She'd spent the ride to the gallery promising herself she wouldn't lose her nerve the minute she came face-to-face with David, but after one shocked look from his green eyes, she was stammering.

Stop that, she told herself sternly, and despite the way her heart was hammering in her throat, she forced a smile to her lips.

"And so," she said, "here I am. You don't mind, do you?"

Mind? *Mind?* David stared at his wife. He wanted to grab her by the shoulders, spin her around and point her toward the door. He wanted to pull her into his arms and kiss her until night faded into dawn. He wanted to corner Corbett and every other arrogant, insufferable M.D. in New York who pretended to know what in hell was happening inside Joanna's head but who obviously didn't know a damned thing more than he did...

"No," he said, very calmly, "I don't mind, Joanna, but are you sure you're up to this?"

Up to having her husband look at her as if he were hoping she'd vanish in a puff of smoke? To seeing the stunned expressions on people's faces as she'd entered the room? To have people say, "Hello, it's wonderful you're up and around,

Joanna'' as she went by and not to have the foggiest notion who they were?

Joanna tried her best not to laugh. Or to cry. Or to do an impossible imitation of both at the same time.

"I'm absolutely up to it," she said with a hundred times more assurance than she felt. "In fact, I think a night out will do me—"

"Joanna? Joanna, is it really you?"

The voice came from a woman who'd stepped out from behind David. She was tall and slender, with pale blond hair cut in a feathered cap that emphasized the perfect structure of her face. Her eyes were pale blue, her lashes dark as soot; her mouth was full and pink. She wore a white silk suit, severely cut yet designed so that it was clear it depended for the beauty of its line not on cut or fabric but on the flawless body beneath.

Joanna smiled hesitantly. She looked at David for help but his face was like stone.

"I'm sorry," she said to the woman, "but I'm afraid I don't..."

"I'm Morgana."

Morgana. David's P.A. This—this Nordic goddess with the flawless face and the marvelous body was Morgana?

Joanna felt a flutter of panic deep in her stomach.

"Morgana," she said, and held out her hand, "how...how nice to see you again."

Morgana seemed to hesitate. Then she took the outstretched hand, leaned forward and pressed her cheek lightly to Joanna's.

"What a lovely surprise." She drew back, looked at David and smiled, and it struck Joanna that the smile seemed strained. "You never said Joanna would be joining us, David."

"No." His eyes held Joanna's. "But then, it's a surprise to me, too."

Joanna flushed and disentangled her fingers from Morgana's. "I only decided to come at the last minute," she lied. "I was just telling David, I...I suppose I should have let him know..."

"Ah-ha! Here we are. Tico, I do believe that this is the lovely lady we have to thank for tonight's marvelous party!"

Joanna swung around and blinked in astonishment. A man and a chimpanzee, dressed in identical tuxedos and trailed by a crowd of onlookers, had appeared at her side.

"You are Mrs. Adams," the man said, "are you not?"

"Why...why yes, I—"

"Joanna," someone called, "yoo-hoo, over here!"

Joanna looked past the man in the tux. A woman with diamonds blazing at her ears and throat was waving at her.

"I'm sorry," Joanna said, "I'm afraid I don't—"

"Tico insisted you weren't Mrs. Adams," the man in the tux said. Joanna turned toward him again and he shot her a blazing smile. "But I said, yes, of course you were, and I was right." He sighed dramatically. "Tico can be so stubborn."

"Jo? Over here. It's so great to see you again. You remember me, don't you?"

Joanna's gaze flew from face to face. "No," she said, "actually, I'm afraid that I—"

"Anyway, Tico was determined to meet you."

"Are you talking about, ah, about the chimp?" Joanna said, looking at the man in the tux again.

"We don't call him that. Not to his face, anyway. It tends to upset him, but then, you know how *artistes* are, they have such delicate..."

"Oh, Joanna," a voice squealed, "I didn't know they'd let you out. How lovely!"

"No one 'let me out'," Joanna said, staring at the blur of faces. "I mean, I'm not sick. Or crazy. I'm just—"

"...egos."

She swung back to the man with the chimp. "Egos?"

"Egos," he said, and nodded. "Delicate ones. All artists are like that, don't you agree?" He stepped closer and breathed into Joanna's face. She pulled back from the scent of...bananas? "Tico, particularly. It truly upsets him to be referred to as a primate."

"As a primate," Joanna repeated stupidly. She looked down at the chimp and it looked back at her.

"Exactly. Oh, do forgive me for not introducing myself. My name is Chico."

"Chico," Joanna repeated. A nervous giggle rose in her throat. "He's Tico? And you're...?"

"Mrs. Adams." A youngish man with his hair sprayed firmly into place shoved forward and stabbed a microphone into her face. "Tom Jeffers, WBQ-TV news," he said with a self-important smile. "Would you care to tell our viewers how you're feeling?"

"Well..." Joanna blinked as the hot lights of a video camera suddenly glared into her eyes. "Well, I'm feeling—"

"Is it true you lost your memory and that you were in a coma for two weeks?"

"No. I mean, yes, but—"

A lush, bleached blonde in a miniskirt jammed a tape recorder under her nose.

"Mona Washbourne, from the *Sun*. Mrs. Adams, what about the rumors that you'd broken all the bones in your body?"

"That's not true. I didn't—"

"How about the plastic surgery they had to do on your face. Any comment?"

"Actually, I—"

"Mrs. Adams." Chico and his tuxedo were all but bristling. "Tico is not accustomed to being kept waiting. If you wish to meet him, you'll have to—"

"All right," David said brusquely, "that's enough."

His arm, hard and warm and comforting, swept around Joanna's waist. She sagged against him, her knees weak.

"My wife has no comment."

"Of course she does," the blonde snapped. "Women are perfectly capable of speaking for themselves. Isn't that right, Mrs. Adams?"

Joanna shook her head in bewilderment. "Please," she whispered, "I don't...I can't..."

A flashbulb went off. Joanna cried out, turned and buried her face in David's chest.

"That's it," he said grimly, and he swung her into his arms.

She made a strangled sound and wound her arms around his neck. Another flashbulb went off in her face. "Bastards," David snarled, and without any apologies he shouldered his way through the mob.

Joanna didn't lift her head until she felt the sudden coolness of the night air on her skin. Carefully, she looked up and peered behind her.

"Oh, God," she moaned.

The crowd had followed them with Chico and Tico, in their matching tuxedos, leading the parade.

"Mrs. Adams!" Chico's high-pitched voice trembled with indignation. "If you don't speak with Tico this instant, he's going to be dreadfully upset!"

"Give him the banana you were saving for yourself," David muttered. "How did you get here, Joanna? Did Hollister bring you?"

She nodded. "He said he'd wait around the corner."

"At least you did something right," he snapped.

A moment later, they were safely inside the Bentley, with the privacy partition up, racing through the darkened streets toward home. Joanna was still in David's arms, held firmly in his lap.

Her heart thumped. He was angry. He was furious! She could feel it in the rigidity of his body, in the way he held her, so hard and close that it was almost difficult to breathe.

"David?" She swallowed dryly. "David, I'm sorry."

In the shadowed darkness, she could just make out the steely glimmer of his eyes as he looked down at her.

"Really," she said unhappily, "I'm terribly, terribly sorry. I never dreamed...I mean, I never thought..."

"No," he growled, "hell, no. You never dreamed. You never thought. Not for one damned minute, not about anybody but yourself."

"That isn't true! I didn't mean to make a scene. It never occurred to me that—"

"What did you think would happen, once the sharks smelled blood in the water?"

"I'm trying to tell you, I never imagined they'd—"

"What in bloody hell was the point in my working my tail off to keep them away from you in the hospital?"

"David, if you'd just listen—"

"And what were you thinking, showing up looking like this?"

Joanna's cheeks flushed. "OK, I suppose I deserve that. I know you prefer me to dress more demurely. It's just that the other night...I thought you said...I realize now, I must have imagined it, but I thought you said you didn't like my hair in a chignon and the kind of dress I was wearing, and...and..."

"Dammit, Joanna, you should never have showed up tonight!"

A rush of angry tears rose in her eyes. She put her hands against David's chest and tried to push free.

"You've made that abundantly clear," she said, "and I promise you, I won't bother you and your little playmate again."

"Playmate? What playmate?"

"Morgana," she said stiffly, "that's what playmate. Damn you, David, if you don't let me go I'll...I'll..."

"What?" he said, and suddenly his voice was low and soft and almost unbearably sexy. "What will you do, Gypsy?"

She tried to tell him, but she couldn't think of an answer. It wouldn't have mattered if she had because his arms tightened around her, his mouth closed on hers, and suddenly he was kissing her as if the world might end at any second.

Joanna hesitated. Then, trembling with pleasure, she buried her fingers in her husband's thick, silky hair and kissed him back.

CHAPTER EIGHT

His mouth was hot, and so were his hands.

And she was burning, burning under his touch.

This is wrong, Joanna's brain shrieked, *it's wrong...*

How could it be wrong, when the searing flame of David's kiss felt so wonderful?

She whispered his name and he drew her even closer, until she was lying across his lap, her hair spilling over his arm, her hands clutching his shoulders desperately as his mouth sought and found the tenderness of hers.

"Open to me, Gypsy," he breathed and she did, parting her lips under the heat of his, moaning softly as he nipped her bottom lip, then stroked the sweet wound with the tip of his tongue.

He groaned and she felt his fingers at the nape of her neck, undoing her zipper, sliding it down until the bodice of her dress fell from her shoulders.

"No," she said, clutching at the silky fabric, "no, David, we can't..."

He cupped the back of her hand, his fingers tangling almost cruelly in her hair as he tilted her head back.

"The hell we can't."

"Hollister..."

"The partition's up. Hollister can't see or hear us." In the dark, his eyes gleamed with an almost predatory brilliance. He bent to her and kissed her until she was trembling in his arms. "This is our own little world, Gypsy. No one can see us. No one even knows we're here." He kissed her again. "And you are my wife."

His wife.

Joanna's breath caught. The simple words were as erotic as any a man had ever whispered to a woman.

And he was right. In the night, surrounded by the anonymity of the city, she felt as if they were alone in the universe.

She sighed with pleasure as he kissed her throat, and then the delicate flesh behind her ear.

"I never forgot the taste of you," he whispered thickly. His kisses were soft as rain, warm as sunlight against her skin. "Like honey. Like cream. Like..."

His lips closed over her silk-encased nipple and she cried out softly and her body arched toward him, a tautly strung bow of consummate sensation.

"Yes," he said, as she whispered his name and wound her arms tightly around his neck.

He groaned softly and shifted her, positioning her over him so that she was kneeling on the leather seat, her short, full skirt draping over his legs like the downturned petals of a flower.

His hand slid under the skirt, cupping her, feeling her wetness, teasing it until finally he hooked his fingers into the fragile crotch of her silk teddy and tore it aside.

Joanna gasped and jerked her head back.

"We're alone, Gypsy," David whispered against her mouth. "There's no one here but you and me. And I want you more than I've ever wanted a woman in my life."

He kissed her, hard, and she responded with an ardor that equaled his. It was what she wanted, too. No preliminaries. No sweet words. Just this, the blinding passion, the urgent need, the coupling that their flesh demanded.

That her heart desired.

Joanna's breath caught.

How could she have been so blind? She loved him. She had always loved him, this stranger who was her husband.

Her injury might have made her head forget him but her soul and her flesh remembered. He was a part of her, he always had been, and now her blood was throbbing his name with each beat of her heart.

"Gypsy?"

He was waiting, waiting for her to give him her answer. And she gave it, blindly, gladly, lifting her mouth to his for the sweet, possessive thrust of his tongue, clasping his face in her hands and dragging it down to hers.

He groaned softly, a primitive sound of triumph and need.

"Unzip me," he said, and she hurried to obey, her hands shaking with the force of her desire.

Her fingertips brushed over the straining fabric of his trousers. She felt the pulsing hardness of his erection.

"Joanna," he said urgently, and his hand moved, his fingers seeking, finding, caressing her secret, weeping flesh.

She was sobbing now, aching for him, empty without him; she had been empty for a long, long time.

"David," she whispered, and her fingers closed on the tab of his zipper...

The Bentley lurched. A horn blared, and the big car lurched again.

Joanna blinked. She pulled back in David's arms. "What was that?"

David cursed softly. "I don't know." His arms tightened around her. "And I don't care."

"No. No, wait..." She lay her palms against his chest. "David, stop."

"Come back here!" His voice was rough with desire; he cupped her face in one hand and kissed her. "I'm crazy with the need to be inside you, Gypsy. I want to feel your heat around me, to hear you cry out my name as you come."

Joanna felt as if she were awakening from a deep, drugged sleep. The Bentley had slowed to a crawl. She turned her head to the window, peered out the dark glass. They were moving through a construction zone; yellow caution lights blinked in the road.

She felt her face grow hot. No one could see in, she knew that. The tinted glass made it impossible. But that didn't keep her from suddenly feeling as if she and David were on display.

His hand stroked over her naked shoulders.

"David," she said, "please..."

His mouth burned at her breast.

"No. Stop it." She began to struggle. "David," she said sharply, "stop!"

He lifted his head. His eyes were dark, almost unfocused; his breathing was ragged. A *frisson* of fear tiptoed down her spine. All at once, her husband seemed more a stranger than ever.

"David." She shoved harder against his chest and shoulders. "Let me go, please."

"Don't be a fool! You know you want this—need this—as badly as I do. Come back here and—"

"No!" She tried to twist away from him but he wouldn't let her. "You don't know the first thing about what I want."

"I know exactly what you want. And you damned well almost got it."

Her hand cracked against his jaw. They stared at each other and then David let go of her and she scrambled off his lap. He turned away and lay his forehead against the cool window glass.

What in hell was the matter with him?

Here he was, a grown man, sitting in the back seat of a limousine with his wife straddling his lap, the bodice of her dress down at her waist and her skirt hiked up to her hips, and if she hadn't stopped him he'd have taken her here, on the cold leather seat, with no more finesse than a boy out on his first date.

And he was angry at Joanna?

God, what a pathetic excuse for a man he was.

She hadn't done a thing. Not one damned thing. She'd simply appeared from out of the blue, looking the way he'd never stopped remembering her, sounding the way she'd once sounded, and against all the rules of logic and reason he'd gone crazy, first with rage and then with lust and all because the terrible truth was that he'd never stopped loving the woman he'd thought he'd married.

For all he knew he might never, ever stop loving her.

What a joke.

He'd called Joanna a fool but if she was a fool, what did

you call a man who was in love with a woman who'd never really existed?

Whoever this Joanna was, once her memory returned, she'd vanish as quickly as she had the first time. And then they'd be right back where they'd been before the accident, two people with nothing in common but his status and their impending divorce.

It would have made things easier if she understood. But what could he tell her? That the loss of her memory had made her a better person? That while she prayed for the return of her memory, he dreaded it?

David drew a shuddering breath. Making love to Joanna would have been like making love to a dream.

It was a good thing she'd stopped him. A damned good thing.

It had probably taken all her courage to show up at the party and he'd repaid that courage by being a selfish bastard.

"Joanna?" He reached out his hand and she slapped it away. "Jo, listen, I know how you feel—"

She turned toward him. He'd expected to see anguish in her eyes, that her mouth—that soft, sweet mouth—would be trembling, but he was wrong.

What he saw wasn't anguish but rage.

"You're truly remarkable," she said bitterly. "First you know what I want, now you know what I feel."

"Jo, I'm trying to apologize. I should never have…"

The limousine pulled to the curb. The engine shut off and the silence of the night settled around them. Joanna glared at him in the darkness.

"If you ever touch me again," she said, "so help me, David, I'll—I'll…"

Her voice broke. The door swung open. He caught a quick glimpse of Hollister's startled face as Joanna shoved past him, ran up the steps and disappeared inside the house.

At five in the morning, David was still sitting in the darkened living room.

He'd been there for hours, ever since they'd come in. His

jacket was off, his tie was gone and the top few buttons of his shirt were undone. His shoes lay beside his chair. There was an open decanter of cognac on the table beside him and a glass in his hand. He wasn't drunk though, God knew, he'd done his best.

Footsteps sounded softly on the stairs.

He rose to his feet and ran his hand through his hair. Then he walked quietly to the door and into the pool of pale yellow light cast by the lamp in the foyer.

"Joanna?" he said softly.

She paused, midway down the stairs. She was wearing a long yellow robe, her hair was caught back in a loose braid, and if she was surprised to see him, it didn't show on her face.

"Hello, David," she said tonelessly.

"Are you all right?"

"I'm fine."

She wasn't. Shadows lay like bruises below her eyes.

"I was just..." He raised his cognac snifter. "Would you like some?"

"No. No, thank you." She lifted both hands to her face and lightly touched her fingertips to her temples. "Actually, I came down for some aspirin. I couldn't seem to find any in my bathroom."

"I'll get you some."

"I'll get it myself, thank you."

Her voice was cool. Don't argue with me, it said, and he decided it might be best to take the hint.

He sighed, went back into the living room and sat down, nursing his cognac, anticipating her return, trying to figure out what to say, hell, trying to figure out what he could possibly do, to convince her he was sorry.

The seconds passed, and the minutes, and finally he put down his glass, stood up and walked back out to the hallway.

"Joanna?"

There was a light at the end of hall. He followed it, to the kitchen. Joanna was standing in front of the open refrigerator, in profile to him. Her body was outlined in graceful brush strokes of light: the lush curve of her breast, the gentle fullness of her bottom, the long length of her legs.

His throat went dry. His hands fisted at his sides as he fought against the almost overwhelming urge to go to her, to take her in his arms and hold her close and say, Don't worry, love, everything's going to be fine.

He cleared his throat.

"Did you find the aspirin?"

She nodded and shut the refrigerator door.

"Yes, thank you. I was just making myself some cocoa."

"Cocoa?" he said, and frowned.

She went to the stove. There was a pot on one of the burners. She took a wooden spoon from a drawer and stirred its contents.

"Yes. Would you like some?"

He shut his eyes against a sudden memory, Joanna at the stove in Connecticut, laughing as she stirred a saucepan of hot milk.

Of course it's cocoa, David. What else would anybody drink when there's a foot of snow outside?

"David?"

He swallowed, looked at her, shook his head.

"Thanks, but I don't think it would go so well with cognac."

She smiled faintly. Then she shut off the stove, took a white porcelain mug from the cabinet and filled it with steaming cocoa.

"Well," she said, "good night."

"Wait." He stepped forward, into the center of the room. "Don't go, not just yet."

"I'm tired," she said in a flat voice. "And it's late. And I don't see any point in—"

"I'm sorry."

Her head came up and their eyes met. Joanna's throat constricted. He looked exhausted and unhappy, and she imagined herself going to him, taking him in her arms and offering him comfort. But there was no reason for her to comfort him, dammit, there was no reason at all!

It was he who'd hurt her, who'd been hurting her, from the minute she'd awakened in the hospital.

Tears stung in her eyes. She blinked hard and forced a smile to her lips.

"Apology accepted," she said. "We've both been under a lot of pressure. Now, if you'll excuse me—"

"Joanna."

His hands closed on her shoulders as she walked past him. She stood absolutely still, her back to him.

She'd been awake all the night, staring at the ceiling and telling herself that what she felt for her husband—what she'd thought she'd felt—had been a lie, that in her confusion and the loneliness that came of her loss of memory, she'd fooled herself into thinking he meant something to her.

And she'd believed it.

Then, why was his touch making her tremble? Why was she fighting the urge to turn and go into his arms?

Stop being a fool, she told herself angrily, and she slipped out from beneath his hands and swung toward him.

"What do you want now, David? I've already accepted your apology." She took a ragged breath. "In a way, I guess some of what happened was my fault."

"No. You didn't—"

"But I did. I showed up uninvited, as you so clearly pointed out. And...and I suppose I should have worn something more in keeping with...with my status as your wife."

"Dammit, Jo—"

"As for what happened in the limousine..." Her cheeks colored but her gaze was unwavering. "I'm not a child, David. I'm as responsible for it as you. I shouldn't have let you—I shouldn't have..."

"Will you listen to me?"

"Why? We have nothing to discuss...unless you want to talk about a separation."

He recoiled, as if she'd hit him again. She couldn't blame him. What she'd said had shocked her, too. She hadn't expected to say anything about a separation, even though that was all she'd thought about for the last few hours.

"What in hell are you talking about?"

"It would be best," she said quietly. "You know we can't go on the way we are."

"You're talking nonsense!"

"Just give me a couple of days to—to find a place to live and—"

His hands clamped down on her shoulders.

"Are you crazy? Where in hell would you go?"

"I don't know." Her chin lifted. "I'll find a place. All I need is a little time."

"You're ill, don't you understand that?"

"I'm not ill. I just—"

"Yeah, I know. You just can't remember." David's eyes darkened. "Forget it, Joanna. It's out of the question."

"What do you mean, it's out of the question?" She wrenched free of his grasp. "I don't need your permission to leave. I'm not a child."

"You're behaving like one."

They glared at each other. Then Joanna slammed the mug of cocoa down on the table, turned on her heel and marched out of the room.

"Joanna?" David stalked after her. She was halfway up the stairs. "Where in hell do you think you're going?"

"Stop using that tone of voice with me." She spun toward him, her eyes flashing with anger. "I'm going to my room. Or do I need your approval first?"

"Just get this through your head," he snapped. "There won't be any separation."

"Give me one good reason why not!"

"Because I say so."

Joanna's mouth trembled. "That's great. If you can't win a fight, resort to typical male tyranny..." Her words tumbled to a halt and a puzzled look came over her face. "Typical male tyranny," she whispered. Her gaze flew to his. "David? Haven't I...haven't I said that before?"

He came slowly up the stairs until he was standing a step below her. "Yes," he said softly, "you have."

"I thought so." She hesitated. "For a minute, I almost remembered...I mean, I had one of those flashes... Did we...when I said that to you, had we been quarreling over the same thing? About—about me leaving you?''

A smile curved across his mouth. He reached out his hand and stroked his forefinger along the curve of her jaw.

''We hadn't been quarreling at all,'' he said in a quiet voice. ''We'd been horsing around beside the pond—''

''In Connecticut?''

He nodded. ''I'd been threatening to toss you in and you said I wouldn't dare—''

''And—and you made a feint at me and I laughed and stepped aside and you fell into the water.''

He was almost afraid to breathe. ''You remember that?''

Joanna's eyes clouded with tears. ''Only that,'' she whispered, ''nothing else. It's—it's as if I suddenly saw a couple of quick frames from a movie.''

He cupped her cheek with his hand. ''I came up sputtering and you were standing there laughing so hard you were crying. I went after you, and when I caught you and carried you down to the pond to give you the same treatment, you said I was a bully and that I was resorting to—''

''Typical male tyranny?''

''Uh-huh.'' His voice grew husky. ''And I retaliated.''

Joanna stared at him. There was something in the way he was looking at her that sent a lick of flame through her blood.

''How?''

His smile was slow and sexy.

''I didn't dump you into the pond. I carried you to the meadow instead.''

''A...a green meadow,'' Joanna said. ''Filled with flowers.''

''...and I undressed you, and I made love to you there, with the sweet scent of the flowers all around us and the sun hot on our skin, until you were sobbing in my arms.'' He cupped her face with his hands. ''Do you remember that, Gypsy?''

She shook her head. ''No,'' she whispered, ''but I wish... I wish I did...''

Silence settled around them. Then David drew a labored breath.

"Go to your room," he said quietly.

Joanna swallowed hard. "That's where I was going, before you—"

"Get dressed, and pack whatever you'll need for the weekend."

Her brow furrowed. "What for?"

"On second thought, don't bother." He smiled tightly. "It seems to me you left the skin you shed in the bedroom closet in Connecticut."

"What on earth are you talking about?"

"We're going away for the weekend. Trust me," he said brusquely, when she opened her mouth to protest, "it's a very civilized thing to do, in our circle."

"I don't care if it's the height of fashion! I'm not going anywhere with you. I absolutely refuse."

"Even if going with me means you might begin to remember?"

She stared at him, her eyes wide. "Do you really think I will?"

Did he? he thought. And if she did…heaven help him, was that what he really wanted?

"David?"

"I don't know," he admitted.

"But you think I might…?"

"Get going." His tone was brisk and no-nonsense as he clasped her elbow and hurried her to her room. "I'll give you ten minutes and not a second more."

"David?"

He sighed, stopped in his tracks halfway down the hall, and turned toward her.

"What now?"

Joanna moistened her lips. "Why do you call me that?"

"Why do I call you what?" he said impatiently.

"Gypsy."

He stared at her and the moment seemed to last forever.

Then, slowly, he walked back to where she stood, put his hand under her chin and gently lifted her face to his.

"Maybe I'll tell you while we're away."

He bent his head to her. She knew he was going to kiss her, knew that she should turn her face away...

His lips brushed softly over hers in the lightest, sweetest of caresses.

The gentleness of the kiss was the last thing she'd expected. Her lashes drooped to her cheeks. She sighed and swayed toward him. They stood that way for a long moment, linked by the kiss, and then David drew back. Joanna opened her eyes and saw a look on his face she had not seen before.

"David?" she said unsteadily.

He smiled, lifted his hand and stroked her hair.

"Go on," he said. "See if you can't find some old clothes and comfortable shoes buried in that closet of yours and then meet me downstairs in ten minutes."

Joanna laughed. It was silly, but she felt giddy and girlish and free.

"Make it fifteen," she said.

Impetuously, she leaned forward and gave him a quick kiss. Then she flew into her room and shut the door behind her.

CHAPTER NINE

THERE'D been a time David would have said he could have made the drive to Fenton Mills blindfolded.

He hadn't needed to check the exit signs to find the one that led off the highway, nor the turnoffs after that onto roads that grew narrower and rougher as they wound deeper into the countryside.

It surprised him a little to find all that was still true.

Even after all this time, the Jag seemed to know the way home.

Except that it wasn't exactly "home" and hadn't been for almost three years.

A young couple who farmed some land up the road from the house were happy to augment their income by being occasional caretakers. They kept an eye on things, plowed the long driveway when it snowed and mowed the grass when summer came, even though David never bothered coming up here anymore.

Sometimes, he'd wondered why he bothered hanging on to the property at all.

His accountant had asked him that just a few months before.

"You get no financial benefit from ownership," Carl had said, "and you just told me you never use the house. Why not get rid of it?"

David's reply had dealt with market conditions, real estate appreciation and half a dozen other things, all of which had made Carl throw up his hands in surrender.

"I should have known better than to offer financial advice to David Adams," he'd said, and both men had laughed and gone on to other topics.

Remembering that now made David grimace.

He'd done such a good snow job on Carl that he'd damned near convinced himself that he was holding on to the Connecticut property for the most logical of reasons.

But it wasn't true.

He'd hung on to the house for one painfully simple, incredibly stupid reason.

It reminded him of a life he'd once dreamed of living with a woman he'd thought he'd loved.

With Joanna.

He'd bought the place years ago, with his first chunk of real money. He had no idea why. This was not the fashionably gentrified part of Connecticut, though the area was handsome. As for the house...it was more than two hundred years old, and tired. Even the real estate agent had seemed shocked that someone would be interested in such a place.

But David, taking the long, leisurely way home from a skiing weekend, had spotted the For Sale sign and known instantly that this house was meant for him. And so he'd written a check, signed the necessary papers, and just that easily, the house had become his.

He'd driven up weekends, with a sleeping bag in the back of his car, and camped out in the dilapidated living room, sharing it from time to time with a couple of field mice, a bat and on one particularly eventful occasion, a long black snake that had turned out to be harmless.

Carpenters came, looked at the floors and the ceiling, stroked their chins and told him there was a lot of work to be done. Painters came, too, and glaziers, and men with specialties he'd never even heard of.

But the more time David spent in the old house, the more he began to wonder what it would be like to work on it himself. He found himself buying books on woodworking and poring over them nights in the study of the Manhattan town house he'd bought for its investment value and its location and never once thought of as home.

He started slowly, working first on the simpler jobs, asking for help when he needed it. Had he undertaken such a restoration in the city, people would have thought him crazy but here, in these quiet hills, no one paid much attention. New Englanders had a long tradition of thrift and hard work; that a man who could afford to let others do the job for him would prefer to do it himself wasn't strange at all.

He found an unexpected pleasure in working with his hands. There was a quiet satisfaction in beginning a job and seeing it through. He learned to plane wood and join floor boards, and the day he broke through a false wall and uncovered a brick fireplace large enough to roast an ox ranked right up there with the day years before when he'd opened the *Wall Street Journal* and realized he'd just made his first million on the stock exchange.

Local people, the ones who delivered the oak boards for the floors or the maple he'd needed to build the kitchen worktable, looked at the house as it evolved under his hands and whistled in admiration. The editor of the county newspaper got wind of what he was doing and politely phoned, asking to do what she called a "pictorial essay."

David just as politely turned her down. Dumped on a church doorstep as a baby, he'd grown up the product of an efficient, bloodless state system of foster child care.

This house, that he was restoring with his own hands, was his first real home. He didn't want to share it with anyone.

Until he met Joanna.

He brought her to the house for a weekend after their second date. The old plumbing chose just then to give out and he ended up lying on his back, his head buried under the kitchen sink. Joanna got down on the floor with him, handing him tools and holding things in place and getting every bit as dirty as he got.

"You don't have to do this stuff, Gypsy," David kept saying, and she laughed and said she was having the time of her life.

By the end of that weekend, he'd known he wanted Joanna not just in his bed but in his heart and in his life, forever. Days later, they were married.

At first, he was wild with happiness. The usual long hours

he spent at his office became less important than being with his wife.

Morgana came as close to panic as he'd ever seen her.

"I don't know what to tell people when they phone, David," she said. "And there are conferences, and details that need your attention..."

He pondered the problem, then flew to the coast for three intensive days with the latest Silicone Valley *wunderkind*. By the time he returned home, the problem was solved.

After a squad of electricians spent a week rewiring the house, a battery of machines came to beeping, blinking life in the attic. Faxes, computers, modems, laser printers, even a high-tech setup that linked David to his New York office by video...

There was nothing he could not do from home that he had not once done in Manhattan, though he still flew down for meetings on Thursdays and Fridays, and always with his beautiful, beloved wife at his side. Sometimes the meetings ran late. Joanna never complained but David was grateful to Morgana, who kept her occupied the few times it happened.

And then, things began to change.

It started so slowly that he hardly noticed.

Joanna suggested they spend an extra day in the city. "I'd really love to see that new play," she said.

An invitation to the opera came in the mail. He started to toss it away but Joanna caught his hand, smiled, and said she'd never been to the opera in her life.

Before he knew it, they were spending five days a week in New York, then the entire week. Joanna met people, made friends, joined committees.

Connecticut, and the simple life they'd enjoyed there, got further and further away.

Morgana, who knew him as well as anyone except his wife, sensed his unhappiness and tried to help.

"You mustn't be so possessive," she told him gently. "A woman needs room to grow, especially one as young as Joanna."

So he backed off, gave her room. But it didn't help. The

gap between them became a chasm. Joanna gave up pretending she liked the country at all. She begged off lazy weekend drives and quiet evenings by the fire. She hinted, then straight out told him she preferred the luxury of their Manhattan town house, and before David knew what was happening, the town house was crammed with ugly furniture and his life was governed by the entries in his wife's calendar.

The girl he'd fallen in love with had changed into a woman he didn't like.

Joanna traded denim and flannel for cashmere and silk. She scorned hamburgers grilled over an open fire in favor of *filet mignon* served on bone china in chic restaurants.

And she'd made it clear she preferred her morning coffee brought to her bedside by a properly garbed servant, not by a husband wearing a towel around his middle, especially if that husband was liable to want to sweeten the coffee with kisses instead of sugar.

David's hands tightened on the steering wheel of the Jaguar. That had been the most painful realization of all, that his passionate bride had turned into a woman who lay cold in his arms, suffering his kisses and caresses with all the stoicism of a Victorian martyr.

Had she worn a mask all along, just to win him? Or had his status and his money changed her into a different person?

After a while, he'd stopped touching her. Or wanting her. He'd made a mistake, and he'd fix it.

Divorce seemed the only solution...

Until last night, when his kisses had rekindled the fire they'd once known and she'd burned like a flame in his arms.

Was that why he'd suddenly decided on coming here this weekend? Not in hopes of jarring her memory, as he'd claimed, but because...

No. Hell, no. He wasn't going to make love to Joanna, not this weekend or any other. He'd brought her to Connecticut because she'd had another of those all-too-swift flashes of memory, and they'd all been connected to this house.

The sooner she remembered, the better. The sooner he could give up his sham of a marriage and get on with his life—

"We'll be there soon, won't we?"

Joanna's voice was soft and hesitant. David looked at her. She was staring straight ahead. The sun was shining on her hair, making it gleam with iridescence.

"Just another few miles," he said. "Why? Do things seem familiar?"

She shook her head. "No. I just had the feeling that we were coming close... What a pretty road this is."

"Yes, it is."

"I like the stone walls we keep passing. Are they very old?"

"Most of them date back to Colonial times. Farmers built them with the stones they cleared from the land as they plowed."

"So many stones... It must have been hard land to cultivate."

"They still say that stone's the only crop that grows well in New England."

She smiled. "I can believe it."

I can't, David thought. We're talking like two characters in a travelog.

"What kind of house is it?"

So much for travelogs. That was the same question she'd asked the first time he'd brought her here, and in that same soft, eager voice. He remembered how he'd smiled and reached for her hand.

"A house I hope you'll love as much as I do," he'd said.

This time, he knew enough not to smile or to touch her, and the only thing he hoped was that this weekend would end her amnesia and his charade.

"It's an old house," he said, and launched into the safety of the travelog script again. "The main section was built in the 1760's by a fairly prosperous farmer named Uriah Scott. His son, Joseph, added another wing when he inherited the house in the 1790's and each succeeding generation of Scotts added on and modernized the place."

"The house stayed in the Scott family, then?" Joanna

sighed. "How nice. All those generations, sharing the same dreams...that must be wonderful."

David looked sharply at his wife. She had said that the first time, too, and just as wistfully. The remark had seemed poignant then, coming from a girl who'd been raised by a widowed father who'd cared more for his whiskey than he had for her; it had made him want to give her all the love she'd ever missed...

What a damned fool he'd been!

"Don't romanticize the story, Joanna," he said with a hollow smile. He glanced into his mirror, then made a turn onto the winding dirt road that led to the house. "Old houses are a pain in the ass. The floors sag, the heating systems never work right no matter what you do to them, there are spiders in the attic and mice in the cellar—"

"Is that it?"

He looked at the white clapboard house with the black shutters, standing on the gentle rise at the top of the hill. It was a small house, compared to the newer ones they'd passed along the way; it looked lonely and a bit weary against the pale Spring sky. The winter had been harsher than usual; the trim would need to be painted as soon as it got a bit warmer and he could see that the winter storms had worked a couple of the slate roof tiles loose.

A bitter taste rose in his mouth.

What had he ever thought he'd seen in this place to have made it magical?

"Yes," he said, "that's it. I'm sorry if you expected something more but—"

"Something more? Oh, David, what more could there be? It's beautiful!"

What in hell was this, a game of *déjà vu*? That was another thing she'd said the first time they'd come here. Later on, he'd realized that it had all been said to please him.

He prided himself on being a man you could only fool once. He swung toward her, a curt retort on his lips, but it died, unspoken, when he saw the enraptured expression on her face.

"Do you really like it?" he heard himself say.

Joanna nodded. "Oh, yes," she whispered, "I do. It's perfect."

And familiar.

She didn't say that, though she thought it. It was far too soon to know if this weekend would jog her memory and there was no point in getting David's hopes up, nor even her own. And she sensed that he was having second thoughts about having brought her here. She was having second thoughts, herself. If she didn't begin to remember after this weekend the disappointment would be almost too much to bear.

"Jo?"

She blinked and looked up. David had parked the car and gotten out. Now, he was standing in the open door, holding out his hand.

"Shall we go inside?"

She looked into his eyes. They were cool and guarded. She had the feeling that he was hoping she'd say no and ask him to turn around and go back to the city. But she'd come too far to lose her courage now.

"Yes," she said quickly, "yes, please, let's go inside."

David wasn't sure what he expected once Joanna stepped inside the door.

Would she clap her hand to her forehead and say, "I remember"? Or would she take one look at the small rooms and the old-fashioned amenities and say that she didn't remember and now could they please go home?

She did neither.

Instead, just as she had all those years ago, she almost danced through the rooms, exclaiming with delight over the wide-planked floors and the windows with their original, hand-blown glass; she sighed over the banister he'd once spent a weekend sanding and varnishing to satin smoothness.

He'd made an early morning phone call to the couple who were his caretakers and he could see that they'd stopped by. The furniture was dusted, the windows opened. There was a pot of coffee waiting to be brewed on the stove and a basket of home-baked bread on the maple table he'd built. A jar of homemade strawberry jam stood alongside and there was a bowl of fresh eggs, butter and a small pitcher of thick cream in the refrigerator.

Joanna said it was all wonderful, especially the fireplaces and the hand pump on the back porch. But she added, with a happy laugh, that she was glad to see there was a modern gas range and real running water and a fully stocked freezer because she wasn't that much of a stickler for the good old days.

And suddenly David thought, but these *were* the good old days. This woman bent over the pump, inelegantly and incongruously attired in a pale gray cashmere sweater, trendy black nylon exercise pants and running shoes... "It's the only comfortable stuff I could find," she'd explained with a little laugh, when she'd reappeared that morning...this woman, with her hair hanging down her back and her face free of makeup, was everything he'd ever wanted, everything he'd thought he'd found when he'd found Joanna.

Dammit, what was wrong with him?

He muttered a short, sharp epithet and Joanna swung toward him.

"What's the matter, David?"

"Nothing."

"But you just said—"

"I, ah, I saw a mouse, that's all."

"A mouse? Where?"

"It ran out from under the sink. Don't worry about it. There are probably some traps in the barn out back. I'll set some out later."

"You don't have to do that. I'm not—"

"I'll show you upstairs," he said brusquely. "You didn't get much sleep last night, Joanna, and this trip has probably been tiring. I think it might be a good idea for you to take a nap."

"Oh, but..." But I'm not tired, she'd almost said.

But being tired had nothing to do with it. He wanted her out of the way for a while; she could hear it in his voice. They'd only just arrived and already he was sorry he'd brought her.

Joanna nodded. "Good idea," she said with a false smile. "You lead the way."

There were three closed doors upstairs. One opened onto a bathroom, one onto a steep flight of steps that led to the attic. The third gave way on a spacious bedroom with exposed beams and a fireplace, dominated by a massive canopied bed...

One bedroom? Only one?

Joanna stopped just inside the doorway. "Oh," she said. "I never thought..."

David understood. "It's not a problem," he said quickly. "There's another bedroom downstairs. I'll be perfectly comfortable there. You go on, Jo. Take a nap. When you get up, we'll go for a drive. I'll show you a little bit of New England. Who knows? Maybe something you see will jog your memory."

"Sure," she said brightly, "that'll be fun."

She shut the door after him. Then she walked to the window, curled onto the wide sill, and stared out at the rolling hills dressed in the tender green of late Spring and wondered why in heaven's name she couldn't just bring herself to ask him, straight out, why they didn't share a bed or even a room.

And if, in fact, they ever had.

Joanna did nap, after a while, and when she awoke, she was amazed to see that there were long shadows striping the room.

She got up, padded across the narrow hall to the bathroom, washed her hands and her face. In the process, she caught a glimpse of herself in the mirror.

Ugh, what a mess! Her hair needed combing, and a touch of lipstick wouldn't hurt. And this silly outfit... There was a wall-length closet in the bedroom, and David had said something cryptic about her not needing to bring anything with her. Maybe there was something in the closet that would look and feel better than this.

She made a soft exclamation of surprise when she looked into the closet. It was filled with clothing, all things she must have bought and all very different from what hung in her closet back in New York. There were jeans and corduroy pants, worn soft and fine with age and washing. Cotton shirts, and sweaters. Sneakers and walking shoes, hiking boots and a pair of rubber things that were as ungraceful as anything she'd ever seen but would surely keep your feet dry and warm in snow.

And there were David's clothes, too. Jeans, as worn as hers. Boots and shoes, sweaters and flannel shirts...

Joanna's throat constricted. They had shared this room, then.

This room. And this bed...

"Jo? Are you awake?"

She spun toward the door, and toward his voice just beyond it. "Yes," she called, and cleared her throat, "yes, David, I am. Just give me a minute and I'll be down."

"Take your time."

Her fingers flew as she pulled off her clothes. She put on jeans, a pale pink cotton shirt and a pair of gently beat-up leather hiking boots that felt like old friends as soon as she got them on. Then she tied a navy blue pullover sweater around her shoulders and brushed her hair back from her face. She found a tube of pale pink lipstick in a tray on the maple dresser, put some on her mouth, and went downstairs.

"Hi," she said brightly, as she came into the living room.

David turned around. "Hi, yourself." His smile tilted as he looked at her. "Well," he said, "I see you found your clothes."

"Uh-huh." She caught her lip between her teeth. "David? What did you mean about me shedding my skin in Connecticut?"

His face closed. "It was a stupid thing to have said."

"But what did you mean?"

"Only that I knew you had a closet filled with stuff to wear."

"Yes, but—"

"What do you feel like having for dinner?"

"Dinner? I don't know. I haven't even thought about—"

"There's a place half an hour or so away that's supposed to have excellent French cuisine."

She laughed. "French cuisine? Here?"

David smiled. "We're not exactly on the moon, Jo."

"Oh, I know. I just meant... I know you're going to think I'm crazy..."

"What?"

"No. Never mind. French is fine." She smiled and gave a delicate shudder. "Just so long as they don't serve—what was that stuff? Goat cheese?"

He laughed, leaned back against the wall, and tucked his hands into the rear pockets of his jeans.

"Goat cheese will be the least of your worries," he said. "Go on, tell me what you were going to say."

She took a deep breath and somehow, even before she spoke, he knew what was going to come out of her mouth.

"You'll laugh, I know, but when I looked in the freezer before... David, what I'd really love for dinner is a hamburger."

It was a mistake.

The whole damned thing was a mistake, starting with the minute they'd left Manhattan straight through to now, sitting here on the rug beside the fireplace in the living room with his wife, his beautiful wife, watching her attack an oversize burger with total pleasure while smoky music poured like soft rain from the radio.

What in hell was he doing? Why was he pretending to listen to what she was saying when he couldn't hear a word because he was too busy thinking how the light of the fire danced on her lovely face?

He forced himself to concentrate. She was telling him a story about one of the woman at Bright Meadows who'd been convinced she'd been born on the planet Pluto.

"...know I shouldn't laugh," she said, licking a drop of ketchup from her finger, "but, oh, David, if you could have heard how serious she was..."

He laughed, because he knew she expected it. But he wasn't

laughing inside, where it counted, because he was too busy admitting that the best thing that could come out of this weekend was that Joanna would remember nothing.

Heaven help him, he was falling head over heels in love with her all over again.

"...asked me where I was born and when I said, well, I couldn't really say because...David? What's the matter?"

David rose to his feet.

"Listen, Joanna..."

Listen, Joanna, we're leaving. That was what he'd intended to say. We're gonna get out of here while the getting's good.

But that wasn't what he said at all.

"Jo," he said, and held out his hand, "will you dance with me?"

Her eyes met his. Color, soft as the pink of a June sunrise, swept into her cheeks. She smiled tremulously, put her hand in his and got gracefully to her feet.

He led her to the center of the room and put his arms around her. There was no pretense, no attempt to pretend that dancing was really what this was all about. Instead, he drew her close against his hard body, his hands linked at the base of her spine. She stiffened and he thought she was going to resist. But then she gave a soft, sweet sigh, looped her arms around his neck and let herself melt into the music and his embrace.

It was wonderful, holding her like this. Feeling the sweet softness of her breasts against his chest, the warmth of her thighs against his. His hand dropped from the small of her back and curved over her bottom. He lifted her against his growing hardness so that she could know what was happening to him.

Joanna made a little sound as she felt him pulse against her. The knowledge that he wanted her was like a song drumming in her blood. He'd wanted her last night, too, but not like this. What had happened in the car had been about lust but this...

This was about love.

She was sure of it, as sure as she could ever be about anything. She loved David, she knew that with all her heart. And he loved her. She could feel it in his every caress.

She drew back in his arms and looked deep into her husband's eyes.

"David?" she whispered.

"Gypsy," he said softly, "my Gypsy," and then his mouth was on hers and his hands were on her breasts and he was drawing her down to the rug in front of the fireplace and into a drowning whirlpool of passion.

CHAPTER TEN

THE wind sighing through the trees and the rain pattering gently against the roof woke David from sleep.

He lay unmoving, struggling to get his bearings in a darkness broken only by the flickering light of the fire on the hearth. Then he felt the sweet warmth of Joanna's body curled into his, smelled the fragrance of her hair spilled across his shoulder, and joy filled his heart.

His wife lay in the curve of his arm, snuggled tightly against him. Her head was nestled on his biceps, her hand lay open and relaxed on his chest. Her leg was a welcome weight thrown over his.

It was the way they'd always fallen asleep after they'd made love, the way it had been in those days so long gone by, days he'd never dreamed of recapturing.

But they had.

Was it a miracle? Or was it some cruel trick of fate? Would his wife stay as she was, even after she recovered her memory…or would she go back to being the cool, acquisitive stranger he'd been about to divorce?

There were so many questions, but there were no answers.

David eased onto his side, slid his other arm around Joanna and drew her close. The last, faint light of the dying fire played across her face, highlighting the elegant bones. She was so beautiful, and never more so than after they'd made love, and he knew that the questions didn't matter, not tonight.

All that mattered was this.

He buried his face in her hair, nuzzling it back from her shoulder, and pressed his mouth gently to the curving flesh. Still asleep, she sighed and snuggled closer.

The scent of her rose to his nostrils, a blend of flowers and sunshine and the exciting muskiness of sex. He kissed her again, his lips moving up her throat and to her mouth.

"Mmm," she said, and stirred lazily in his arms.

His hand cupped her breast.

"David," she sighed, and linked her hands behind his neck.

He smiled against her mouth. "Hello, sweetheart."

"Was I asleep?"

"We both were." He bent his head and kissed her with a slow, lazy thoroughness. "It's late."

"Mmm."

"The fire's almost out, and it's pitch black outside."

"Mmm."

"We should go to bed."

Joanna's laugh was soft and wicked. "What do we need a bed for? I thought we managed just fine."

His hand slid down her body and slipped between her thighs. She made a small sound of pleasure as he cupped her warm flesh.

"Better than fine," he murmured. "But now I want to make love to my wife on soft pillows and under a down comforter."

"That sounds wonderful." Joanna's smile tilted. "David? We…we shared a bedroom, didn't we? Before my accident, I mean."

She felt him stiffen in her arms and she cursed herself for ruining this perfect night. But instead of rolling away from her, as she'd half expected, he sighed and lay back with her still in his arms.

"Yes," he said, after a long silence. They had shared a bedroom, they'd shared everything…a long time ago. But he couldn't tell her that, not without telling her all the rest, about the divorce, about how different she was now… "Yes," he said again, "we did."

Joanna rolled onto her stomach, propped her elbows on the rug and her chin in her hands and looked down into her husband's face.

"Even back in the city?"

"Yes, even there." He reached up his hand and gently

stroked her tangled curls back from her face. "We used to share my bedroom until…"

"Until what? Why did we…why did we decide on separate rooms? And when? Have we been sleeping separately for a long time?"

He sighed. Trust this new Joanna to come up with some damned good questions. And trust him not to have any good answers.

The truth was that they'd never "decided" on separate rooms; it had just happened. He'd started spending occasional nights in his study, stretching out on the leather sofa after working late. The excuse he'd offered himself, and Joanna, was that he hadn't wanted to wake her by coming to bed after she was asleep.

And Joanna had said there was no reason for him to spend the night on a sofa when they had a perfectly usable extra bedroom available. She'd been thinking of converting it into something more to her tastes, she'd added with a brittle smile. Would that be all right?

Of course, he'd told her, and not long after that he'd come home and found Joanna's clothes gone from the closet in the master suite and what had been the guest room remade into something that looked like a bad layout from a trendy magazine…

"David?"

He looked at his wife. She was still waiting for an answer and he decided to give her the only one he could. An honest one, as far as it went.

"I can't really tell you, Jo." Gently, he clasped her shoulders and rolled her onto her back. "It just happened. I'm not even sure exactly when."

"I asked you once if we'd been unhappy," Joanna said, "and you gave me the same kind of answer. But we weren't happy, David, I know we weren't."

In the shadowy darkness, he could see the tears welling in her eyes. For one wild moment, he thought of telling her the truth. No, he'd say, hell, no, we weren't happy…

But they had been, once. And they could be again. The thought surged through him, pushing aside everything else.

"I mean," she said, her voice trembling, "if we were sleeping in separate beds, leading separate lives..."

David didn't hesitate. He crushed his mouth to hers, silencing her with a deeply passionate kiss.

"That's over," he said fiercely. "No more sleeping apart, Gypsy. And no more separate existences. You're going to be my wife again."

"Oh, yes, that's what I want. I..." She caught herself just in time. I love you, she'd almost said, I love you with all my heart.

But the idea of being the first to say the words frightened her. It was silly, she knew; there was nothing frightening about telling your husband you loved him—unless you couldn't recall him ever saying those three simple words to you.

"I want to be your wife," she whispered instead, and she smiled. "And I want to know why you call me Gypsy. You said you'd..." Joanna's breath caught. "David! What are you...?"

"I'm getting reacquainted with my wife," he murmured, his breath warm against her breasts and then against her belly. "Your skin is like silk, do you know that? Hot silk, especially here."

She cried out as he buried his face between her thighs and kissed her, again and again, until she was sobbing with the pleasure of it. And after she'd shattered against his mouth he rose over her and buried himself deep inside her, riding her with deep, powerful thrusts until she climbed that impossible mountain of sensation once again, then tumbled from its peak as he exploded within her.

There were tears on Joanna's cheeks when David at last withdrew from her. He tasted their salinity as he kissed her.

"Don't cry, sweetheart," he whispered.

"I'm not," she said, and cried even harder, "I'm just so happy."

He kissed her again as he gathered her into his arms.

"Joanna," he said, "I..."

He bit back the words just in time. Joanna, he'd almost said, I love you.

But how could he tell her that? It was too soon. He couldn't even let himself think it, not so long as he both knew and didn't know the woman he held in his arms.

"I'm glad," he said softly, and then he rose to his feet and carried her up the stairs to their bedroom, where he held her tightly in his arms all through the rest of the long night.

When he awoke again, it was morning.

The rain had stopped, the sun was shining, a warm breeze was blowing through the open window.

And the wonderful scent of fresh coffee drifted on the air.

David rose, dragged on a pair of jeans and a white T-shirt. He made a quick stop in the bathroom. The shower curtain was pulled back and there was a damp towel hanging over the rod.

Barefoot, thrusting his fingers into his hair to push it back from his forehead, he made his way down to the kitchen.

Joanna was turned away from him, standing in the open back door so that the morning sunlight fell around her like a golden halo. Her hair was still damp and fell over her shoulders in a wild tumble. She was barefoot and wearing a pair of incredibly baggy shorts that sagged to her knees and an old cotton shirt of his that still bore traces of the buttercup yellow paint they'd used to paint the pantry years before.

My wife, he thought, my beautiful wife.

His heart felt as if it were expanding within his chest. Back in his college days, during one of the all-night bull sessions that had been, in their way, as valuable as any class time, a guy who'd had one beer too many had said something about there being a moment in a man's life when everything that was important came together in a perfect blend.

David knew that this was that moment. No matter what the future held, there would never be an instant more right than this one, with Joanna standing before him, limned in golden sunlight, after a night spent in his arms.

"Good morning," he said, when he could trust his voice.

She spun toward him. He saw the swift race of changing emotions on her face, the joy at seeing him warring with the morning-after fluster of a woman new to a man's bed, and he smiled and held out his arms. She hesitated for a heartbeat, and then she flew into his embrace.

"Good morning," she whispered, tilting her face up to his. He accepted the invitation gladly and kissed her. She sighed and leaned back in his arms. "I didn't wake you, did I?"

He shook his head and put on a mock ferocious scowl. "No. And I want to talk to you about that."

Joanna's brows rose. "What do you mean?"

"I like it when you wake me." The scowl gave way to a sexy grin. "Very much, as a matter of fact. There I was, all ready to greet the day with a special pagan ritual—"

"A special pagan...?"

"Uh-huh. And I had all the ingredients, too. The sun, the bed, my ever-ready male anatomy..."

"David!" Joanna blushed. "That's awful."

His arms tightened around her. "You didn't think so last night."

"Well, no. I mean, *that's* not terrible. I mean..." She giggled, then dissolved in laughter. "Sorry. I never thought about your 'ever-ready male anatomy.' I just thought about being desperate for coffee."

"I'm desperate, too." He lifted her face to his. "For a kiss."

Joanna sighed. "I thought you'd never ask."

Their kiss was long and sweet. When it ended, David kept his arm looped around Joanna's shoulders while he poured himself a cup of coffee.

"What do you want to do today?"

She smiled up at him. "You pick it."

"If it's left to me to choose," he said, bending his head to hers and giving her another kiss, "we'll go back to bed and spend the day there."

She blushed again, in a way he'd all but forgotten women could.

"That doesn't sound so terrible to me," she whispered.

David put down his cup, took Joanna's and put it beside his.

"I don't want to tire you out, Jo," he said softly. "I know, I know, you haven't been ill. But you've been under a lot of stress."

Joanna put her arms around his neck. "Making love with you could never tire me out. But I have to admit, I'd love to see more of the countryside. It's so beautiful here."

"Beautiful," he agreed solemnly, and kissed her again. When the kiss ended, he knew he had to do something or he'd end up carrying her back to bed and keeping her there until neither of them had the strength to move. So he took a deep breath, unlinked her hands from around his neck, and took a step back. "OK," he said briskly, "here's the deal. I'll shower, then we'll go get some breakfast."

"I can make breakfast. We've got those lovely eggs in the fridge, and that fresh butter and cream..."

"Lovely eggs, huh?" David grinned. "OK. Just give me ten minutes to shower... Come to think of it, that was another thing I'd planned."

"What?"

"Well, first the pagan ritual to greet the day, then a shower together." A wicked gleam lit his green eyes. "What the heck. I had to do without the pagan bit but there's no reason to ditch both ideas."

"David?" Joanna danced away as he reached for her. "David, no! I already took a shower. See? My hair is...David? David!" Laughing, she pounded on his shoulders as he caught her in his arms, tossed her over his shoulder, and headed for the stairs. "You're crazy. You're impossible. You're..."

But by then, they were already in the shower, clothes and all, and she shrieked as he turned on the water and it cascaded over them. And somehow, in the process of stripping off each other's soaked clothing, somehow, they ended up worshiping the sun and each other, after all.

"Tell me again," Joanna said, wiping a ribbon of sweat from her forehead with the back of her hand, "we really used to do this?"ᵗ

David nodded. They were standing in the midst of what looked like an automotive graveyard.

"All the time," he said absently. "Hey, is that what I think it is?"

"Is what what you think it is?" Joanna followed after him as he wove his way through the rusting hulks of what had once been cars.

"It is," he said triumphantly. He plucked something from the nearest pile of rubble and held it out. "Ta-da!"

"Ta-da, what?" She poked a finger at the thing. It looked like a metal box with pipes attached. "What is that?"

"A heat exchanger. If you knew how long I've been looking for one..."

Joanna laughed. "Yeah, well, to each his own, I guess. This place is amazing. To think anybody would save all this junk..."

"It's not junk," David said firmly, "it's a collection of what may be the best used sports car parts in the northeast."

"Uh-huh."

"And this heat exchanger, woman, is the catch of the day."

"Will it fit the Jag?"

"Of course."

"Do you need it?"

David shot her a pitying look. "I don't. But you thin-blooded types do. Come on, give me your hand and we'll go pay the man for..." He turned toward her. "That's just what you used to ask me," he said softly.

"What?"

"Do you need it?" He lay his hand along the curve of her cheek. "We bought the Jaguar together. And we worked on it together. And we had a great time, but you used to tease me, you'd say that you didn't know buying the car meant we'd have to poke through—"

"—through every junkyard in the lower forty-eight," Joanna said, "with long-term plans for Hawaii and Alaska." Her eyes flew to his. "That's what I used to say, wasn't it?"

David nodded. "Yes."

"I can hear myself saying it." Her throat worked dryly. "David? What if…what if my memory comes back and—and spoils things?"

Her fear mirrored his, but he'd be damned if he'd admit it.

"Why does it have to?" he said, almost angrily.

"I don't…I don't know. I just thought—"

"Then don't think," he said, and kissed her.

They stopped for lunch at a tiny diner tucked away on a narrow dirt road.

"No menus," David said, waving away the typed pages the waitress offered. "We'll have the chili. And two bottles of—"

"—Pete's Wicked Ale," Joanna said, and smiled. She waited until the woman had gone to the kitchen before she leaned toward David.

"Do I like chili?" she whispered.

He grinned. "Does the woman like chili? I used to say you must have been born south of the border to love chili as much as you did."

"Is that why you call me Gypsy? Because you teased me about being born in Mexico?"

His grin faded. "Gypsies don't come from Mexico. You've got your continents mixed."

"I know. But every time I try to get you to tell me why you call me that name, you change the subject." She reached across the scarred tabletop and took hold of his hand. "So I figured I'd back into the topic."

"Cagey broad," David said, with a little laugh. He sighed and linked his fingers through hers. "There's no mystery, Jo. It just…" It hurts me to remember, he wanted to say, but he didn't. "It just happened, that's all."

"How?"

"Because that's how I thought of you." He looked at her and smiled. "As my wild, wonderful Gypsy."

"Was I wild?"

"Not in the usual sense. You just had a love for life that…"

"Ale," the waitress said, putting two frosted bottles in front of them. When she'd left, David leaned forward.

"You were nothing like the women I knew," he said softly. "You didn't given a damn for convention or for the rules."

"Me?" Joanna said, her voice rising in a disbelieving squeak as she thought of her conventionally furnished town house, her chauffeured car, her clothing, her life as it was mirrored in her appointment book.

"The first time I saw you, you were wearing hiking boots, wool socks, a long wool skirt and a lace blouse with big, puffy sleeves that narrowed at your wrists."

"Leg-o'-mutton," she said, frowning. "Where was I? At a costume party?"

He laughed. "You were sitting at the reception desk at Adams Investments."

Joanna's eyes rounded. "I was what?"

"Our regular receptionist had called in sick. She said she had the flu and she'd be out for the week. So Morgana phoned a temp agency and they sent you over."

"Morgana," Joanna said, frowning.

"Yeah." David chuckled. "She didn't want to hire you, she said you didn't fit our image."

He paused as the waitress served their chili.

"And I agreed with her," he continued, after they were alone again. "But we were desperate. There were six people in the waiting room, the telephones were ringing off the walls, and who else could we have come up with on such short notice?"

Joanna smiled. "It's so lovely to be hired because you're wanted," she said sweetly. "Thank you, David." She spooned some chili into her mouth and rolled her eyes in appreciation.

"Good?"

"Wonderful. So, go on. I looked like a refugee from a thrift shop but you hired me anyway, and—"

"And I offered to drive you home that night, because we worked late."

"I'll bet that didn't thrill Morgana."

He frowned. "You don't like her very much, do you?"

"Don't be silly," she said quickly. "How could I not like her when I hardly know her?"

David reached across the table and took Joanna's hand. "She was a good friend to you, Jo. After you and I married, you felt a little, well, lost, I guess. And Morgana did everything she could to help you settle in."

"Settle in?"

"Yeah." He cleared his throat. "It was all new to you. Living in Manhattan, entertaining..."

"You mean, I was the poor little match girl who married the handsome prince and went to live in his luxurious castle," she said softly.

"No. Hell, no." His fingers tightened on hers. "You weren't accustomed to..." *To money. To status. But, by God, she'd grown accustomed quickly enough...*

"I understand." Joanna sighed. "And I'm sure Morgana was terrific. I don't know why..." She sighed again and gave him a little smile. "Actually, I do know. It's because she's so gorgeous and she gets to spend so much time with you. For a while there, I even thought—I imagined..."

"Morgana is my right-hand man," David said, dragging his thoughts from where he wished they hadn't gone. "She's efficient, and very bright, and I trust her implicitly. But that's all she is and all she ever has been."

"I'm glad to hear it," Joanna said, and smiled. "Go on. Tell me what happened when you drove me home."

He felt some of the sudden tension ease from his muscles. He grinned, let go of her hand and picked up his spoon.

"What do you think happened?"

"What?"

"Nothing."

"Nothing?"

"Cross my heart. You were the soul of propriety, and so was I."

"Good." She laughed. "For a minute there, you had me thinking that—"

"I wanted you so badly that I ached."

Color swept into her face. "Right away?"

"Oh, yeah." He spooned up some chili. "The minute I saw you. But I did the right thing," he said, deadpan. "I waited until our second date."

"Our second…" Joanna's color deepened. "Tell me you're joking!"

"We made love," he said, smiling into her eyes, "and it was incredible."

"Incredible," she whispered, as fascinated as she was shocked.

"Uh-huh. And a few days after that, we got married."

Joanna's spoon clattered against the tabletop.

"Got married? So fast? After knowing each other, what, two weeks?"

"Ten days," he said, making light of it, wishing he could tell her how he'd proposed with his heart in his mouth for fear she'd turn him down and walk out of his life…and how, not even a year later, he'd wished she had.

Ten days, Joanna thought. Well, why not? It couldn't have taken her more than ten minutes to have fallen in love with David.

But what about him? She'd been the soul of propriety, he'd said. What had happened? Had he wanted her to sleep with him—the ever-ready male anatomy at work—and when she'd refused, had he made an impulsive offer of marriage and ended up regretting it?

Was that what had gone wrong between them? Had he simply looked at her across the breakfast table one morning and asked himself what in hell she was doing there?

When the sexual excitement of this weekend was over, would he look at her and think that same thought again?

"Jo?" David reached for her hand. "What is it? You're so pale."

Joanna forced a sickly smile to her lips. "I think…I think you were right when you said I shouldn't overdo." Carefully, she pushed her bowl of chili away. "Would you mind very much if we went back to the house now?"

He was on his feet before she'd finished speaking. "Let's go," he said, tossing a handful of bills on the table. She stood up, he put his arm around her and the next thing she knew, he was carrying her from the diner.

"David, put me down. This is silly. You don't have to pick me up every time I—"

He kissed her, silencing the quick flow of words in a way that made her heartbeat stutter.

"I love holding you," he whispered fiercely. "I'd hold you in my arms forever, if I could."

He tucked her gently into the car, buckled her seat belt, then got behind the wheel and drove slowly home. And all the time, she wondered if he'd meant what he'd said, if it would last or if everything that had happened between them would end when the weekend did.

He insisted on lifting her from the car and carrying her into the house.

"I'm going to take you upstairs and put you to bed," he said. "And when you're feeling better, I'll make us some supper."

"Don't be silly. I feel better already. I'll cook."

"What's the matter? Afraid of trying my extra-special canned chicken soup?"

Joanna laughed. "At least let me lie down in the living room so I don't feel like a complete invalid."

"Deal." He lowered her gently to the couch and smiled at her. "And since you're feeling better, I'll let you have a vote."

"A vote on what?"

David grinned. "Raise your hand if you want us to stay right where we are for the rest of the week."

Her eyes widened. "Do you mean it?"

"Scout's honor."

"Oh, that would be wonderful. But your office..."

"They'll manage." He leaned down, brushed his mouth lightly over hers. "Lie right there and don't you dare move an inch. I'll put up the kettle for some tea and phone Morgana." He smiled. "She'll probably be delighted at the chance to run things without me for a while."

Joanna smiled and lay her head back as David made his way to the kitchen.

Had she ever been so happy in her life?

Even the fears she'd had just a little while ago didn't seem quite so awful now. There was more to her relationship with David than sex. There had to be. That he wanted to stay here with her, away from the rest of the world, was wonderful.

Regaining her memory no longer seemed as quite as important as it had. What mattered now was getting her husband to admit that he loved her.

"Jo?"

She looked up. David was coming slowly toward her, his smile gone.

"David, what's wrong?"

"Nothing, really." He squatted down beside her and took her hand in his. "I mean, it's not like it's the end of the world or anything…"

"But?"

He sighed. "But Morgana said she'd been just about to phone me. I've been working on this project for the Secretary of Commerce… Hell," he said with an impatient gesture, "the point is, the White House has become interested."

Joanna gave a little laugh. "The White House? Are you serious?"

David nodded. "The Secretary wants a meeting. Gypsy, there's no way I can put him off."

"Of course not."

"If it was anything else…"

"David, you don't have to explain. I understand."

"Look, we'll go back to New York tomorrow, I'll meet with the Secretary and his advisors and next weekend, we'll drive up again and stay for the week. OK?"

Joanna nodded. "Sure."

She hoped she sounded as if she meant it but as she went into David's arms and lifted her face for his kiss, there was a hollow feeling in the pit of her belly, as if she knew in her heart that they would not be returning to this house again.

CHAPTER ELEVEN

THE servants in the Adams town house were in the habit of taking their mid-morning coffee together.

It was Mrs. Timmons's idea and though it made for a pleasant start to the day, it was a ritual that had less to do with congeniality than with efficiency. The housekeeper had found she could best organize the day with Ellen and Hollister seated opposite her at the kitchen table.

But she could see instantly that that wasn't going to work this morning.

Nothing was going according to schedule. And she had the feeling that nothing would.

The Adamses had returned from their weekend outing late last night. Mrs. Timmons had been watching the late news on the TV when she'd heard them come in and she'd risen from the rocking chair in her bedroom cum sitting room off the kitchen, hastily checked her appearance in the mirror, and gone out to see if she were needed.

What she'd seen had made her fall back into the shadows in amazement.

There was Mr. David, carrying his wife up the stairs. He'd done that the day he'd brought her home from the rehabilitation center, but this...oh, this was very different.

Mrs. Adams's arms were tightly clasped around her husband's neck. They were whispering to each other, and laughing softly, and halfway up the stairs Mr. David had stopped and kissed his wife in a way that had made Mrs. Timmons turn her face away. When she'd dared look again, the Adamses were gone and the door to Mr. David's bedroom was quietly clicking shut.

Now, at almost ten in the morning, the door to that room had yet to open. Neither of the Adamses had come down for breakfast and Mr. David had even foregone his daily run.

"Never happened before," Hollister said, dipping half a donut into his coffee.

"Of course it has," Mrs. Timmons said briskly, "it's just that you weren't here at the beginning."

"The beginning of what?"

"I'll bet she means when they were first married," Ellen said with a giggle, "when they were still newlyweds. Isn't that right, Mrs. Timmons?"

Ellen blanched when the housekeeper fixed her with a cold eye. "Isn't this your day for organizing the clothing for the dry cleaner?"

Hollister came to Ellen's defense.

"She was only picking up on what you'd just said," he began, then fell silent under that same stern gaze.

"And you," Mrs. Timmons said, "are supposed to be polishing the silver."

Hollister and Ellen looked at each other, shrugged their shoulders and pushed back their chairs.

"We can take a hint," Hollister said with quiet dignity.

Mrs. Timmons began clearing the dishes. "Good," she said grumpily. But after the door had swung shut and she was alone in the kitchen, she stood still.

She had worked for David Adams for many years and she'd come to respect him. She supposed, if pressed, she might even admit she'd developed a certain liking for him.

"Damnation," she muttered.

The truth was that she'd come to think of him as if he were a kind of son. Not that she'd ever let him or anyone else know it. That would not have been proper.

But if Joanna Adams, who had broken his heart once, had somehow got it into her head to break it twice...

The coffee cups clattered against each other as Mrs. Timmons all but jammed them into the sink.

No. It was just too impossible to contemplate.

Not even fate could be that cruel.

*   *   *

Upstairs, in the master bedroom suite, David stood gazing down at Joanna, who lay fast asleep in his bed.

The weekend, and the night they'd just spent together, had been wonderful.

His gaze moved slowly over his wife. She was lying on her belly, her head turned to the side so that he could see her dark lashes fanned down over her cheek. The blanket was at her hips, exposing the long, graceful curve of her back. Her hair, black as night against the white linens, streamed over her shoulders.

He loved her, he thought. Lord, he loved her with all his heart.

If only he dared tell her so.

Joanna sighed. She stretched lazily, rolled onto her back and opened her eyes. Her face lit when she saw her husband, standing beside the bed.

"David," she whispered, and without any false modesty or hesitation, she raised her arms to him.

He came down to her at once, his freshly pressed suit, crisp white cotton shirt and perfectly knotted silk tie be damned, and folded her tightly into his embrace.

"Good morning," he said softly, and when she smiled, he kissed her.

It was a slow, gentle kiss but almost instantly he felt his body begin to react to the warmth and sweetness of hers.

"Mmm," he whispered against her mouth, and he moved his hand to the silken weight of her breast. His fingers stroked across her flesh and then he bent his head and drew her nipple into his mouth.

Her response was swift and exciting. She made a soft little sound that was enough to drive him crazy all by itself but when she arched toward him, murmuring his name, her hand cupping the back of his head to bring his mouth even harder against her, it was almost his undoing.

With a groan, he lifted his head, kissed her lips, and drew back.

"I can't, darling," he said softly. "My meeting is in less than an hour."

Joanna smiled and smoothed his hair back from his forehead.

"I understand."

"I should have told Morgana to say I couldn't make it."

"No, you shouldn't. It's OK, David. Really. I do understand."

David took her hand and brought it to his lips. "I'll be back
as soon as I can."

She sat up, put her arms around his neck, and kissed him.
"I'll be waiting," she whispered.

He stroked his hand down her cheek. Then he stood,
straightened his clothes and headed for the door while he could
still force himself to leave.

This Joanna, this woman he'd fallen in love with all over
again, couldn't be a temporary aberration. She had to be real,
and lasting.

He could not suffer her loss again.

Not even fate could be that cruel.

Morgana picked up the papers on David's desk and squared
them against the blotter though she'd done the same thing only
moments before. She looked at the onyx desk clock.

David was late. Twenty minutes late. That wasn't good.

He was never late. Not for the past couple of years, at any
rate; not since he'd stopped being cutesy-cozy with his adoring
little minx of a wife.

Morgana's sculpted lips pressed together with distaste. David's marriage had almost marked the end of all her plans.
Until then, it had only been a matter of time before he'd have
realized what she, herself, had known from the first day she'd
come to work for him.

She and David were meant for each other.

One look, and she'd fallen deeply in love. David...well, he
was a man. It took men longer to realize such things. For a
long while, it had been enough that he'd found her the best
P.A. he'd ever had. Morgana had taken each compliment on
her efficiency, her dedication, and clutched them to her heart.

Soon, she had told herself, soon he'd know.

Instead, he'd been captivated—seduced—by a common piece of baggage from out of nowhere.

Morgana shot a look of pure venom at the photo of Joanna that stood on the corner of David's desk.

"Just look at her," she muttered under her breath.

The hair, blowing in the wind; the oversized denim shirt tucked into torn jeans. And that smile, that oh-so-innocent smile.

Morgana smiled, too, but her smile was as frigid as a January night.

At first, it had seemed an insurmountable problem. It had been bad enough that David had gotten married. But when he'd begun spending less and less time at the office, Morgana had suffered in silence, watching as her plans for a future with him began to fall apart.

Until one day, she'd seen her chance.

David had made a comment, a light one, really, something about not wanting to overwhelm his bride with the pressures of her new life. But Morgana had sensed real concern behind his words.

All smiles, she'd offered to befriend Joanna.

The girl had been so young. Stupid, really. She'd swallowed everything Morgana fed her, hook, line and sinker.

"I'm so happy for you," Morgana had purred. "It must be so wonderful, up there in Connecticut. Why, David's missed several important meetings because he didn't want to leave. He didn't tell you? No? Oh, dear, I suppose I shouldn't have said anything."

"No," Joanna had replied, "no, I'm glad you did. I surely don't want to interfere in David's life."

After that, it had been easy. A few woman-to-woman chats about things like David's status. His position. His importance on the national and international scenes. His need to entertain, to network with his peers.

"But why hasn't he told me these things?" Joanna had said pleadingly, each time Morgana worked around to the topic, and Morgana sighed and said, well, because he loved her and he was afraid of making too many demands on her too soon.

"Perhaps if you were the one to suggest that you'd like to make some changes," Morgana had said in her most kindly way. "I mean, if David thought you wanted to move back to the city, mingle with his old crowd, if he saw you beginning to adapt yourself to his sort of life...that would please him so, Joanna, and he wouldn't have to feel guilty about asking *you* to change for *him*, do you see?"

Morgana's heels tapped briskly across the Italian tile floor of David's office as she headed out the door to her own desk. It had been as simple as striking a match to start a fire. Joanna made changes, David reacted with disappointment, Joanna— the stupid girl—reacted by making even more changes, and the fire grew larger.

It had been difficult, watching David's growing distress, but it was for the best. His marriage was an error; it was up to Morgana to make him see that.

Finally, he had.

He'd come in one day, called Morgana into his office. Grim-faced, he'd told her that he and Joanna would be getting a divorce.

Morgana had made all the right sounds of distress and concern, even though she'd wanted to throw her arms around him and shout for joy. But she'd told herself she had only to bide her time, that once the divorce was over, she could carefully offer consolation.

Her jaw clenched as she sat down at her desk.

And then Joanna had her accident. If only that taxi hadn't just hit her a glancing blow, if only it had done a proper job...

Morgana took a trembling breath. She put her hands to her hair and smoothed the pale strands.

This had been a long, and terrible, weekend. When she'd gotten the call from David, telling her he was in Connecticut, she'd known immediately that the little slut had seduced him again. It was there in his voice, that soft hint of a male who had been pleasured.

And in that instant, Morgana had known she could no longer wait to see if Joanna's memory would come back, that she'd have to take action if she wanted the fire that she'd started to consume that interfering little bitch.

She would not lose David again. She'd worked too hard to let that happen.

"Good morning."

She looked up. David was coming through the smoked-glass doors toward her. A smile curved across her mouth. How handsome he was. How much she adored him.

"Good morning," she said in her usual, businesslike manner. "There have been some calls for you. I put the memos on your desk." She rose and hurried after him as he went into his office. "A couple of faxes came in from Japan during the night, nothing terribly urgent. Let's see, what else? John Fairbanks phoned to see if you could make lunch today. I said you'd call him when you came in. Oh, and the Mayor's office wanted you to—"

"What time are they coming in?"

Morgana looked blank. "Who?"

"The Secretary and his people." He yanked out his chair, sat down, and began to leaf through the stack of memos and faxes. "Didn't you say something about noon?"

Morgana frowned. What was the matter with her? Yesterday, all she'd thought of was that she had to get David back into his real life and away from his wife.

Now, suddenly remembering how she'd accomplished that, she scrambled for words.

"Oh," she said, "oh, that..."

David looked up at her. His hair was neatly combed, he was clean-shaven, his shirt and tie and suit were impeccable...but she could see beyond all that, she could see the satiation in his face, she could almost smell the damnable stink of that woman.

"Yes," he said impatiently, his voice politely echoing hers, "that. When are these guys supposed to put in an appearance? I don't much feel like cooling my heels today, Morgana."

"They called a few minutes ago," Morgana said quickly, "and changed the time to one o'clock."

That would do it. By one, she'd have David up to his eyeballs in work. Thoughts of his little wife would be relegated to the back burner, where they belonged. And by six or seven, when Morgana suggested she phone out for supper…

"Hell," David muttered, looking at the onyx clock. He ran his hand through his hair. "All right, then, let's not sit around and watch dust settle. Get your notebook and we'll deal with these faxes."

Morgana smiled happily. "Yes, David."

By noon, David had his jacket off and was deep in work.

Morgana sent out for sandwiches. He nodded his thanks and ate what she'd ordered without comment.

At ten of one, she excused herself, and went out to her desk, dialed the phone company and said she thought her telephone might be out of order and would they please ring her right back?

When her phone rang, she picked it up, said thank you, then hung up. She waited a couple of minutes before going into David's office.

He looked up from his desk. He was scowling. A good sign. It surely meant that he was engrossed in his work.

"David, that was a call from Washington. The Secretary sends regrets but he can't make it today."

"Damn!" David tossed down his pen. "You'd think they'd have called sooner."

"Well," Morgana said apologetically, "you know how these people are."

"To think I rushed all the way back to the city for this…"

"But it's a good thing you did," Morgana said quickly. "Just look at all the work you've done."

"Yeah." He pushed back from his desk. "Terrific."

Something in his voice made her scalp prickle. "You know, you never did answer that letter that came in last week from—"

"I suppose, as long as I'm here, I might as well put the rest of the day to good use."

Morgana smiled. "Exactly. That letter…"

David wasn't listening. He'd pulled his telephone toward him and he was dialing a number.

"This is David Adams," he said. "I'd like to speak with Doctor Corbett."

"David," Morgana said urgently, "there's work to do."

David held up his hand. "Corbett? I'm fine, thank you. Look, I've been thinking... Do you have some time free this afternoon, Doctor? I really need to talk to you."

"David," Morgana hissed, "listen—"

"Half an hour from now, in your office? Yes, that's fine. Thanks. I'll be there."

David hung up the phone and got to his feet. He grabbed his suit jacket from the back of his chair and put it on as he walked to the door.

"Where are you going?" Morgana demanded. "Really, David..."

"Joanna's just the way she used to be," he said, and smiled at her. "She's...hell, she's wonderful! Do you remember what she was like, Morgana?"

Morgana's mouth whitened. "Yes," she said, "I do."

"What occurred to me was...I know it sounds crazy, but maybe that blow to the head changed her personality."

"Honestly, you can't believe that."

"Why not? Something's happened to change her." He smiled again, even more broadly. "I've got to talk to Corbett about it. Maybe he can shed some light on things."

"David, no! I mean, that's crazy..."

He laughed. "No crazier than me falling in love with my wife all over again. I'll see you tomorrow." He grinned. "Or maybe I won't. Maybe I'll whisk Joanna off to Paris. Hell, who knows what will happen? I'm beginning to think that anything is possible."

Morgana stared at the door for long minutes after he was gone. Then, her mouth set in a thin, hard line, she collected her jacket and her purse and left the office on the run.

Joanna sat on the delicate, silk-covered sofa in her own living room and wondered if it was possible to feel more out of place than she felt at this moment.

Morgana, an unexpected visitor, sat in an equally delicate chair across from her. In her ice blue, raw silk suit, with her blonde hair perfectly arranged and her hands folded in her lap, she looked completely at home.

Joanna, caught in the midst of trying to bundle most of the contents of her clothing closet for the Goodwill box, knew she looked just the opposite. She glanced down at her jeans, dusty from her efforts, and her sneakers, still bearing grass and mud stains from the weekend in the country. Her hair was a mess, with some of the strands hanging in her eyes. Her hands were grungy and she saw now that she'd broken a nail...

Quickly, she laced her fingers together but it was too late. Morgana was looking at the broken nail as if it were something unpleasant she'd found on her dinner plate.

"You really need to see Rita," she said.

Joanna cleared her throat. "Rita?"

"Yes. The girl who does your nails. You have a standing appointment, hasn't anyone told you?"

"No. I mean, yes, I know I do but I haven't...I mean, the thought of going to a nail salon seems so weird."

Joanna took a breath. This was ridiculous. This was her house. Morgana was her guest. An uninvited one, at that. There was no reason to feel so...so disoriented.

"Morgana," she said, and smiled politely, "would you care for some tea?"

"Thank you, no."

"Coffee, then? It's Mrs. Timmons's afternoon off, and Ellen's out running errands, but I'm perfectly capable of—"

"No."

"A cool drink, then?"

"Joanna." Morgana rose in one graceful movement and dropped to her knees before Joanna. "My dear," she said, and clasped Joanna's hands in hers.

"Morgana," Joanna said with a nervous laugh, "what is this? Please, get up."

"Joanna, my dear Joanna." Morgana's sympathetic blue

eyes met Joanna's wary violet ones. "I've felt so badly for you, ever since that dreadful accident."

"I don't want to talk about the ac—"

"And for David, too."

"Morgana, really, get up. You're making me uncomfort—"

"He told me today why you went away for the weekend. That you'd both hoped the time in the country might help you recover your memory."

It was a shot in the dark, but an accurate one. Joanna flushed. "He told you that?"

"Oh, yes. David and I are very close, Joanna. Surely you remember...well, no, I suppose you don't."

"I know that he thinks very highly of you," Joanna said cautiously.

"Of course he does." Morgana squeezed her hand. "But it's you I'm thinking of now, my dear."

"I don't...I don't follow you."

Morgana sighed and got to her feet. "You were intimate with David this weekend, Joanna."

Joanna blanched. "How did you..."

"He told me."

"David told you...?" Joanna shot to her feet. "Why? Why would he tell you something so...so personal about us?"

"We're very close, I've told you that. And perhaps he was feeling guilty."

"Guilty?" A chill moved over Joanna's skin. "Guilty about what?"

"Are you sure you're up to this? Perhaps I've made a mistake, coming here. I wrestled with my conscience all day but—"

"I feel strong as an ox. Why should my husband have told you that he and I...that we were together this weekend? And why should he have felt guilty about it?"

Morgana's teeth, very tiny and very white, closed on her bottom lip. "Because he's done a cruel thing to you, and he knows it." She took a deep breath. "I can't stand by and see him do it. You see, Joanna, David intends to divorce you."

Joanna felt the blood drain from her face. "What?"

"He should have told you the truth weeks ago. I tried to convince him. So did his attorney, but—"

"His attorney?"

"Yes." Morgana clasped Joanna's hands. "You must be strong, dear, when I tell you this."

"Just tell me," Joanna said frantically, "and get it over with!"

"The day of your accident," Morgana said slowly, "you were on your way to the airport. You were flying to the Caribbean, to get a divorce."

Joanna pulled her hands from Morgana's. "No! I don't believe you. I asked David about our marriage, he never said—"

"He listened to the doctors, who said it was vital you have no shocks to your system."

"I don't believe you. It isn't true..."

Joanna's desperate words halted. She looked at Morgana and then she gave a sharp cry of despair, and spun toward the window and the sad little garden beyond.

It *was* true. Every word. What Morgana had just told her made a terrible kind of sense.

David's unwillingness to bring her home from the hospital. His coldness. His silence. His removal.

Their separate rooms...

But their rooms hadn't been separate this weekend.

"I suppose," Morgana said kindly, as if she'd read Joanna's thoughts, "that it's difficult to accept, especially after the intimacy of the past weekend." She sighed. "But if you could only remember the past, you'd know that...well, that sex was all you and David ever had together. It's what led up to your marriage in the first place."

Joanna looked at her. "What do you mean?"

"Surely you know that David is a man with strong appetites. There have been so many women... They're in his life for a while and then, poof, they're gone. And then he met you. You were so young..." Morgana struggled to keep the anger and hatred from her voice. "He's a moral man, in his own way. I suppose, afterward, he felt an obligation." Morgana smiled pityingly. "Unfortunately, it wasn't love. Not for David."

Joanna's legs felt as if they were going to give out. She made her way to the couch and sat down.

"He said things this weekend," she whispered while the tears streamed down her face, "we planned things..."

"Yes, I'm sure. He was full of regrets for what had happened in Connecticut. I was blunt, I said, 'David, it's your own fault, you shouldn't have listened to the doctors, you should have told Joanna the truth, that your marriage had been an impetuous mistake and you were in the process of ending it...'"

And, with dizzying swiftness, Joanna's memory returned.

"Oh, God," she whispered, "I remember!"

Pictures kaleidoscoped through her head. She saw herself coming to New York from the Midwest, looking for a new life and finding, instead, the only man she would ever love.

David.

He was almost ten years older and he moved in such exalted circles... It was hard to imagine him taking notice of someone like her.

But he had, and on their very first date, Joanna had fallen head over heels in love.

She remembered the passion that had flamed between them, how she, the girl her friends had teasingly called the eternal virgin, had gone eagerly to his bed soon after they'd met.

Oh, the joy of his proposal. The excitement of flying to Mexico to get married, the honeymoon in Puerto Vallarta, the weeks of happiness and ecstasy...

And then the slow, awful realization that she wasn't what David had wanted at all.

He'd never said so. He was too decent. But it was a dream that could not last and the signs of its ending had been easy to read.

David had given up his everything. His friends. His charities. He stopped going to the office, saying he preferred living in Connecticut but Joanna knew that everything he'd done was based on his conviction that she wouldn't fit into the sophisticated life he led in the city.

When Morgana offered her help, Joanna leaped at the chance to salvage her marriage.

What she needed, Morgana told her, was a life of her own, a life that would make David see her as more than just a woman he was responsible for but as someone as proficient in her sphere as he was in his.

"A man of his energies needs challenge to perform at his best, my dear," Morgana said. "By devoting so much time to you, he cheats himself. You must develop interests of your own. Show him you're equal to the position he holds in the world. Perhaps if you joined some clubs, or sat on some charity committees, you'd learn how to organize this house, how to look…"

Morgana clamped her lips together but it was too late.

"You mean," Joanna asked in a choked voice, "he's embarrassed by the way I look?"

"No, not at all," Morgana quickly replied.

Too quickly. Joanna understood that "embarrassed" was exactly what she'd meant.

But nothing she'd tried had been enough to halt the collapse of the marriage. David had grown more distant. The bed that had once been a place of intimacy and joy became the cold setting in which they ended each day by lying far apart until finally, Joanna had salvaged what little remained of her pride by moving into a separate room. Eventually, David had suggested divorce. Joanna had agreed. It had all been very civilized, though the day she'd set out for the airport and the legal dissolution of her marriage she'd been so blinded by tears that she hadn't seen the oncoming taxi until it was too late…

The memories were almost too painful to bear. Joanna buried her face in her hands while Morgana stood over her.

"Poor Joanna," she crooned. "I'm so sorry."

Joanna lifted her tear-stained face. "I can't…I can't face him," she whispered, "not after…"

It was difficult for Morgana to hide a smile of triumph.

"I understand," she said soothingly.

"I don't want to be here when David gets back. I don't want to see him ever again." Joanna grasped Morgana's hands. "Please, you must help me."

"Help you?"

"I have nowhere to go. I don't really know anyone in this city...except you."

Morgana frowned. Time was of the essence. She had to get Joanna out of here before someone showed up. Luck had been with her, so far. The maid and the housekeeper were out; the chauffeur was among the missing, too.

But David...David could come home at any minute.

She made a quick decision. "You can sleep on the pull-out sofa in my living room until we work out the details."

"Oh, no, I couldn't impose."

"Nonsense. Go on, now. And I suppose you'd best leave a note."

"A note?"

"Yes. Something clear and concise, so David understands why you've gone." *So he knows you've left him deliberately, so that he doesn't scour the streets, trying to find you...*

"But what shall I say?"

"Just the truth, Joanna, that you've recovered your memory and you wish to proceed with the divorce."

Joanna nodded. Still, she hesitated.

"Morgana? I'm almost ashamed to admit it but when I first heard David talk about you, I was...I was jealous."

"Of me?" Morgana's smile felt stiff. "What nonsense, Joanna. David's never even noticed that I'm a woman."

But he would notice it, at long last, she thought as Joanna left the room.

Finally, *finally*, she was about to take her rightful place in David Adams's life.

CHAPTER TWELVE

"DAVID," Morgana said, "you must calm down."

"How the hell can I calm down?" David, who had been pacing the floor of his office for the past ten minutes, swung toward Morgana. "It's a week since Joanna disappeared. A week, dammit! And all these damned private investigators are no closer to finding her than they were when I first hired them!"

"Getting yourself all upset won't help."

"I am not getting myself all upset," he snarled, "hell, I'm already upset!" He strode to the triple window and looked out. "Look at the size of that city! Jo could be out there anywhere, alone and hurt and in God only knows what sort of trouble."

"She's not in trouble, and she didn't disappear. She simply left you, David. I mean," she added quickly, when he swung toward her, "that's what you told me. You said she wrote a note."

"Yeah, but what does that prove? She'd been ill. She'd been in an accident. She'd hurt her head..." His face, already pale beneath its usual tan, seemed to get even whiter. He kicked the chair out from behind his desk, sighed and sank down into it. "If only I knew she was OK."

"She is."

"You don't know that."

But I do, Morgana thought smugly, *I surely do*. Joanna Adams was as well as could be expected for a woman who moped around Morgana's apartment all day, looking as if she'd lost her best friend.

It was definitely time to get her out from underfoot. Joanna thought so, too; Morgana had come home two days ago and found her unwelcome boarder with her suitcase packed. She was moving into a hotel, Joanna had said, and though Morgana's first instinct had been to applaud, common sense had prevailed.

If Joanna were on her own, there was no telling what might happen. Suppose she changed her mind and decided to confront David? Or suppose she and David simply bumped into each other? Manhattan was a big island, jammed with millions of people and the odds on that happening were small but still...

Morgana's brain had recoiled from the possibilities. She had to keep Joanna on ice just a little longer. So she'd thought fast and come up with a story about David cutting off Joanna's credit cards and bank accounts.

"The bottom line," she'd said with a gentle smile, "is that you'll just have to stay here a little while longer, dear."

What could Joanna have done but agree?

The only problem was that things weren't going quite as Morgana had expected. She'd assumed David would be distraught, yes, but not...what was the word to describe his behaviour the last several days? Disturbed? Upset?

Frantic, was more like it. He'd gone half crazy when he learned his wife had left him, calling the police, hiring private detectives...

And brushing off all Morgana's attempts to offer comfort.

She looked at him now, sitting behind his desk with his head buried in his hands. It was ridiculous, that he should mourn the loss of a girl as common as Joanna.

"Ridiculous," she muttered.

David's head came up. "What's ridiculous?"

Morgana flushed. "That—that the police haven't found her yet."

David sighed wearily and scrubbed his hands over his face. He hadn't slept more than an hour at a time since he'd come home to find Joanna gone and exhaustion was catching up with him.

"Jo left a note...it means she's not technically a missing

person. If it wasn't for her having amnesia, they wouldn't bother looking at all.''

"She doesn't have amnesia, not anymore. She remembered everything."

David's eyes narrowed. "How do you know that, Morgana?"

"Well…" She swallowed dryly as she searched for the right words. "Well, you said that was in the note. That she'd gotten her memory back."

"Yeah, but what does that mean? What does she remember?" He put his hands flat on his desk and wearily shoved back his chair. "Corbett says memory sometimes returns in bits and pieces. For all I know, she doesn't remember the things that matter."

A look came over his face that made Morgana's stomach curdle.

"Honestly, David," she snapped, "one would think *you'd* remember the things that matter, too."

The look he gave her all but stopped her breath.

"Maybe you'd like to explain that," he said with sudden coldness.

Morgana hesitated. Well, why not? It might be time for a little straight talking, if she could do it with care.

"I mean," she said, "that you seem to have forgotten that your marriage to Joanna was always doomed."

"Doomed?" David rose to his feet. "What in hell gives you that idea?"

"David, don't let your irritation out on me!"

"I just want a simple answer to a simple question, Morgana. Why would you think my marriage had been doomed?"

Morgana's lips pursed. "Honestly, you act as if I weren't privy to the divorce proceedings. And to the years that led up to them. I know, better than anyone, how badly things had gone for you and Joanna."

David's mouth thinned. "You weren't privy to how much I loved her," he said coldly. "As for the divorce proceedings…that was behind us."

"After she'd lost her memory, of course, but—"

"Memory be damned!" He slammed his fist on the desk. Morgana jumped, and papers went flying in all directions. "I love her, do you understand? Even if she'd recovered her memory, there was no reason to think we couldn't have worked things out. Corbett made me see that. I'd loved the woman Joanna had once been, I loved the woman she'd become... Hell, there had to have been a reason she'd changed during our marriage. And I came home that day, knowing it was time to tell her the truth and to tell her that, together, we could find the answers..."

He turned away sharply and his voice broke. Morgana hesitated. Then she went slowly to where he stood and put her hand on his back.

"David," she said softly, "you've got to accept what's happened."

"I don't know what's happened, don't you understand?"

"Joanna remembered. And when she did, she knew she wanted just what she'd wanted before the accident, to be free of you—"

She cried out as he swung around and grabbed hold of her wrist.

"How do you know that?"

Morgana stared at him. "Because...because that's the way it was," she stammered. "You told me—"

"Never."

"You did! You said she wanted a divorce."

"I said we'd agreed on a divorce." David's eyes were cold as the onyx clock on his desk as they searched Morgana's face. "I never said Jo wanted to be free of me."

"Well, I suppose I just assumed..." Morgana looked at his hand, coiled around hers. "David, you're hurting me."

"Hell," he muttered. He let go of her wrist and drew a ragged breath. "I'm sorry. I don't know what I was thinking."

"It's all right. I understand."

"If only I'd gotten home earlier."

"You mustn't blame yourself."

"If only the maid or the housekeeper had been there."

"David, please. Try and relax."

"Even Hollister was gone. He had to pick that damned afternoon to get the oil changed in that miserable car."

"Oh, David, my heart breaks for you. If there were only something I could... What are you doing?"

David shrugged on his jacket. "I'm going home. It's better than pacing a hole in the floor."

"Oh, don't! Let me make us some tea."

"I need an hour's sleep more than I need tea. You might as well take the rest of the day off, too."

"But it's only midafternoon. We can't just abandon the office!"

He smiled. "Trust me, Morgana. We can."

"But..."

It was useless to protest. He was gone.

Morgana walked around David's desk and sat down in his chair. Her mouth twisted.

Damn Joanna! She might have been gone but she wasn't forgotten. And she was an ever-present threat, so long as she remained in New York. She didn't belong here. She never had. She wasn't sophisticated enough, or clever enough, or beautiful enough. Not for the city and not for David.

Joanna belonged back in whatever hick town she'd come from.

Morgana's grimace became a smile. She shoved back the chair and marched to the door.

And the sooner, the better.

Morgana's apartment held the deep silence of midafternoon.

"Joanna?" She slammed the door and tossed her purse and briefcase on a chair. "Joanna, where are you? We have to talk."

Not that she'd give the little slut the chance to talk. She'd simply hand the girl a check, tell her to buy herself a one-way bus ticket, and that would be that.

Life would return to normal. To better than normal, because now David would need solace.

And Morgana would be there to offer it.

What was that?

Her heart began to hammer as soon as she saw the note propped against the toaster in the kitchen. The quiet and that folded piece of white paper filled her with foreboding.

She opened the note, smoothed it carefully with her fingers.

Dear Morgana,
You've been so kind but I can't go on imposing. This morning, I remembered a small cache of money I'd tucked away. I'm going home to get it and then...

"No," Morgana whispered. She crumpled the note in her hand. "No," she said, her voice rising to a wail, and she raced from the apartment.

It didn't take Joanna very long to find what she was looking for.

The couple of hundred dollars she'd squirreled away more than a year ago was in her night table, right where she'd left it. She'd put the money aside last year, to buy David a special birthday gift...

As if that would have changed anything.

Her eyes misted and she rubbed them hard with the heel of her hand. It was stupid, thinking about that. Those days were over and gone. Now, what she had to do was concentrate on the future.

And on slipping out of the house as quietly as she'd slipped in.

It was foolish, she knew, but she didn't want to see anybody. Her timing was right. At this hour on a Friday, Mrs. Timmons would be out marketing. Ellen and Hollister would be in the kitchen, eyes glued to their favorite soap operas.

Joanna made her way quietly down the stairs. The house lay in midafternoon shadow, adding to its natural gloom. She shuddered and thought that she would not miss these over-furnished, cold rooms.

The only thing she'd miss was David, and that was just plain stupid. Songs by the truckload had been written about the pain of unrequited love but in the real world, how could you go on loving someone who didn't love you?

Before the accident, she'd come to terms with that fact. She'd accepted the truth of their impending divorce, and she would again. Her weepiness this past week, her anguish at the thought of losing her husband...it was just a setback, and perfectly understandable in light of all that had happened to her, first the amnesia and then the shock of her recovery, and in between that long, wonderful weekend...

No. It hadn't been that at all. The weekend had been a lie. And she could never forgive David for that, for what he'd stirred in her heart while she'd lain in the warmth of his arms...

The front door swung open just as she reached it. Startled, Joanna jumped back, expecting to see Mrs. Timmons's dour face.

But it wasn't the housekeeper who stood framed in the doorway, it was David.

They stared at each other, the both of them speechless. Joanna recovered first.

"Hello, David," she said. He didn't answer but he didn't have to. The look on his face was far more eloquent than words. He was glaring at her, his amazement giving way to repressed rage. "I—I suppose you're surprised to see me."

Surprised? He was stunned. He was a man who'd never been at a loss for words in his life but at this moment, he was damned near speechless and torn by half a dozen conflicting emotions, all of them warring to get out.

Anger, born of a week's worth of pain and fueled by the way Joanna was looking at him, as if he was the last man on earth she'd ever wanted to see, won out.

"Where in hell have you been?"

Joanna winced. "You don't have to yell, David, I'm not deaf."

"Thank you for the information." A muscle jumped in his cheek. "Now answer the question. Where have you been?"

"I didn't come here to quarrel," she said carefully.

"No?"

"No."

David slammed the door behind him. He took a step toward her and she held her ground through sheer determination.

"Why did you come here, then? To see if I'd torn the wallpaper as I climbed the walls while I tried to figure out if you were dead or alive or maybe just sitting in an alley someplace, singing *Hey Nonny Nonny* while you wove flowers into your hair?"

Color swept into her cheeks. "I am perfectly sane. I've told you that before."

"Yeah?"

"Yeah," she said, and this time when he moved toward her she couldn't keep from taking a quick step back because if she hadn't, they'd have been nose to nose. Or nose to chest, considering the size of him...

"Well, lady, you sure could have fooled me."

Joanna's chin lifted. "I didn't come here to be insulted."

"Fascinating." He unbuttoned his jacket and slapped his hands on his hips. "You didn't come here to quarrel. You didn't come to be insulted. Near as I can figure, that only leaves us with a couple of thousand other possibilities. Are we going to go through them one by one or are you going to tell me how come you decided to honor me with your presence?"

It took a few seconds to get enough moisture into her mouth so she could swallow.

"I came to get something."

"Something?"

"Yes."

David folded his arms over his chest. "I never much cared for Twenty Questions to start with, Joanna, and I find I'm liking it less and less as this conversation goes on."

"It isn't a conversation, it's an inquisition!"

His smile was quick and chill. "No, it's not. Not yet, anyway, but if I don't start getting some straight answers it's sure as hell going to become one."

Joanna folded her arms over her chest, too.

"I came to get some money I'd put..."

She bit her lip. Hollister and Ellen had materialized in the hallway and were staring at them both with wide eyes. David frowned and swung around, following her gaze.

"Well?" he barked. "What do you want?"

"Nothing, sir," Hollister said quickly. "We simply heard the door slam, and then voices..." He looked at Ellen. "Well, uh, we'll just go be getting back to the kitchen."

"You do that," David said coldly. "Better still, go for a walk. Or a drive. Just leave us alone."

Hollister nodded, grabbed Ellen's arm and hustled her away. Joanna, trying to take advantage of the interruption, headed for the door. David reached out and clamped his hand around her wrist.

"Let go," she demanded.

"The hell I will. You were about to explain why you came here."

"I told you, I'd put away some money. I came to get it." Her chin lifted. "I admit, it was yours to begin with but I—"

David cursed, with an eloquence that made her blush.

"Your money? My money? What kind of garbage is that? Money is money, that's all. It always belonged to the both of us."

"I only meant that I'd saved this on my own."

"And what, pray tell, do you need this little 'nest egg' for?"

Joanna licked her lips. "To leave town,"

"Leave town," David repeated. His voice was flat but the muscle was jumping in his cheek again. "As in, cut and run without having the decency to face me and tell me you were leaving me?"

"I *did* tell you," Joanna said, wrenching out of his grasp. "I left you a note."

"Oh, yeah, you certainly did. 'Dear David, My memory came back and I want the divorce.' Yours Very Truly..."

"I didn't say that," she snapped, her cheeks flaming.

"No," he said coldly, "not the 'Yours Very Truly' part but you might as well have."

"David, this is senseless. I told you, I didn't come to argue."

"Right. You came for money you'd squirreled away, I suppose for just such an occasion, so you could do a disappearing act if the going got tough."

She moved so fast that her fist, slamming into his shoulder, was a blur.

"Hey..."

"You...you rat!" Her eyes, black with fury, locked on his. "I saved that money so I could buy you a carburetor for your last birthday!"

David's face went blank. "A what?"

"A carburetor. That—that thing you kept drooling over in that stupid car parts catalog, the Foley or the Holy..."

"Holley," he said in a choked whisper. "A Holley carb."

"Whatever. You had this dumb thing about just ordering it from the catalog, all this crazy male macho about it being better to stumble across it yourself in some stupid, dirty junkyard..."

"It isn't male macho, it's simple logic," David said with dignity, "and what were you doing, buying me a Holley carb in the first place? It sure as hell didn't go with your image."

"No," Joanna said, and all at once he could see the anger drain from her face. "It didn't. But then, just before your last birthday I was still fool enough to think—to hope—that maybe buying you a gift would remind you of how things had once been for us..."

She stared at him, her mouth trembling, despising herself for what she'd almost blurted out, that she loved him, that she would always love him...

A choked sob burst from her throat. Eyes blinded with tears, she turned away. "Goodbye, David. I'll let you know where to send my things. On second thought, you can give them away. Maybe the Goodwill people want—"

She cried out as he hoisted her unceremoniously into his arms and stalked into his study.

"David, are you crazy? Put me..."

He dumped her on her feet, slammed the door shut behind them, and glared at her.

"You're not going anywhere until we've had this out," he said grimly.

"We have nothing to talk about."

"No?"

"No."

"What was all that, about you caring how things once were between us?"

Joanna's shoulders slumped. "I was just babbling. Besides, it doesn't matter anymore."

"The hell it doesn't!" He caught her face in his hand and forced her eyes to meet his. "Does it really matter to you, how things used to be?"

She stared at him, warning herself not to let go, to hang on to what little remained of her self-respect...but it was too late. The words were there, bursting from her heart and her lips.

"Damn you, David," she cried, "I'll always care!" Color stained her cheeks, giving her a wild, proud look. "Do you feel better, now? Wasn't it enough that I couldn't live up to your standards?"

"What the hell are you talking about? What standards?"

"Your wealth. Your status. Your friends. You married me without really thinking about whether or not I'd fit into your life, and then you woke up one morning and realized that I didn't."

"You mean, I woke up one morning and discovered that my beautiful Gypsy had changed into a...a..." David let go of her, flung up his arms and paced across the room. "I don't know how to describe what you'd become! A woman who cared more about other people than about me, who was determined to turn this damned house into a mausoleum, who didn't want me to touch her—"

His words faded way. He looked at her, and suddenly Joanna could see the anguish in his eyes.

"Why, Jo? Why did you turn to ice whenever I tried to make love to you? More than anything else, that damn near killed me."

"Because...because..." Joanna took a deep breath. It was a moment for truth, and she would see it through. "Because I was ashamed of...of how I was, whenever we...we made love."

David stared at her in disbelief. "Ashamed? My God, why?"

Joanna's head drooped. Her voice came out a whisper. "She never said anything, not about that. I'd never mentioned—I would never talk about something so intimate." She laced her hands together to stop their trembling. "But...but she'd hinted. About certain things that I might do or say that would seem coarse..."

David crossed the room with quick strides. "Who?" he said through his teeth. "Who hinted?"

"I did try, David. To do what she said. To be the right wife for you."

"Who told you these things, Joanna?" But with gut-wrenching swiftness, he knew, and he could feel the blood heating in his veins. "Who told you that you weren't what I wanted in a wife?"

"Morgana," Joanna whispered. "She tried so hard to help me make myself over, but it was useless."

David's arms swept around her. "Listen to me," he said. "And look at me, so you'll know that what I'm about to tell you is the truth." He waited until she raised her head and then he took a deep breath. "I never wanted you to change, Gypsy. I loved you, just as you were."

"But Morgana said..."

"She lied."

"Why? Why would she have lied, David? She was so kind to me. Even this week, when I had nowhere to go, she took me into her apartment..."

David's eyes darkened with rage. "You spent this week

with Morgana? I was tearing this miserable city upside down to find you and she had you tucked away all the time?''

His voice was cold as stone, and just as hard. It sent a shudder down Joanna's spine.

''Yes. After she told me about the divorce, after I remembered everything…'' Joanna caught her breath. ''Did you say you'd tried to find me?''

David drew her closer. ''I went crazy this past week,'' he said gruffly. ''Don't you know how much I love you?''

Joanna sighed. She lifted her arms and looped them around his neck.

''No,'' she said, with a little smile. ''You're just going to have to tell me.''

''For the rest of our lives,'' David said, and just then the door burst open.

''Mr. David?'' Mrs. Timmons said, ''are you…?'' Her eyes widened. ''Mrs. Adams. I didn't know you'd come back, ma-'am. I'm terribly sorry to disturb you, but—''

Morgana pushed the housekeeper aside and came sweeping into the room.

''David,'' she said importantly, ''I've seen Joanna, and I think you should know…'' Her face turned white with shock but she recovered quickly. ''She's here already, I see. David, I don't know what she's told you but I assure you, it's all lies!''

David put his arm around Joanna's shoulders. The green chips of sea ice that were his eyes told the whole story.

''If you were a man,'' he said softly, ''I'd beat the crap out of you and smile while I did it.''

''Please, David, I can explain—''

''Get out!''

''This snip of a girl isn't for you. She's…she's…''

David let go of Joanna and took a step forward. ''You lying bitch! If I ever see your face again, I won't be responsible for my actions. Now, get out of this house and out of our lives or so help me, I'll throw you out!''

Morgana drew herself stiffly erect. ''You'll regret losing me some day, but it will be too late then. I'm giving you one last chance to come to your senses—''

She cried out as Mrs. Timmons grasped the back of her collar and hustled her out of the room. The door slammed shut. There was a cry of outrage, then the sound of the front door opening and closing, and then there was silence.

''David?'' Joanna looked up at her husband. ''Do you think she's all right?''

David drew his wife into his arms. ''I don't really care,'' he said. His mouth twitched. ''Yes, I'm sure she's fine. But after this I'll think twice about ever crossing Mrs. Timmons.''

Joanna laughed softly and linked her hands behind his neck. ''Have I told you lately that I love you, Mr. Adams?''

David smiled. ''Welcome home, Mrs. Adams,'' he said softly and then, for long, long moments, there was no need for either of them to say anything at all.

EPILOGUE

Five years later

"KATE? Benjamin? Where are you?"

Joanna sighed as the sound of childish giggles spilled from the old-fashioned country kitchen behind her.

"Your daddy's car is going to be coming up that road any minute and if you want to be ready to go outside and greet him, you'd better show yourselves and let me get your boots on." She waited. "OK," she said, "I'm going to count to three and then whoever's not standing right in front of me is going to have to wait in the house. One. Two. Th—"

"Here I am, Mommy."

A little girl with dark hair and eyes the color of violets raced like a whirlwind into the living room.

"That's my girl," Joanna said. She hugged her daughter close and gave her a big kiss. "Now, where's that brother of yours?"

"Here, Mommy," her son sang out, and hurled his chubby, three-year-old self into her outstretched arms. "Daddy's gonna be here soon."

"That's right, darling. Sit down and let me get these boots on."

Benjamin collapsed on the carpet next to his twin sister.

"He's gonna bring me a truck," he said importantly, "with big wheels and a horn that goes beep."

Joanna laughed. Her son was the image of his father, with his dark hair and his green eyes. He had his father's passion, too, for anything on wheels.

"There we go," she said. "Almost ready. Just let's button you guys up…"

"Ugh," Kate said.

"Ugh," Benjamin echoed.

"Yes, I know, but it's cold out and there's lots and lots of snow…"

A horn sounded outside the snug Connecticut farmhouse. The children screeched happily and flew out the front door, trundling down the steps clumsily in their boots and snowsuits just as a black Land Rover pulled up. The door opened and David stepped out.

"Hey," he said, grinning as he squatted down and opened his arms. The children raced into them and he kissed them both, then scooped them up, one in each arm. "Did you miss me?"

Kate laughed. "Silly Daddy. You were only gone one day." Then she leaned forward and planted a wet kiss on his cheek. "I missed you every minute," she whispered.

"Me, too," Benjamin said, and delivered an equally sloppy kiss on the other side of his father's face. Then he craned his neck and peered over David's shoulder. "Did you bring my truck, Daddy?"

"Let's see," David said thoughtfully, as he set his children on the ground. "Did I bring Benjamin a truck? Well…I think maybe I did." He pulled a gaily wrapped package from the Land Rover and handed it to his son, who promptly sat down in the snow and began ripping it open. "There might even be something in here for Kate…yup, by golly, there is." Wide-eyed, his daughter accepted a box almost as big as she was. She plopped herself down beside her brother and set to work. "And there might even be one more thing in here some-place…"

For the first time, David looked up at the porch where Joanna stood framed in the doorway. After nine years of marriage and two babies, she was more beautiful than ever and his heart did what it always did at the sight of her, rose straight up inside his chest until he felt as if he could float.

"Hello, wife," he said softly.

Joanna smiled. "Hello, husband."

He mounted the steps slowly, his eyes never leaving hers, and when he reached the porch she went into his arms and kissed him.

"A year," she whispered, her lips warm against his cold cheek. "That's how long it seems since you left yesterday morning. A year or maybe a month or—"

David kissed her again. "I know. The next time I have to go into the city, you and the kids are coming with me."

"That sounds like a wonderful idea. How's the apartment?"

"Fine. Mrs. Timmons sends her best." David drew back, then held out the package. "I brought you something."

Joanna looked at the box and smiled. "Do I get to guess what it is?"

"Sure. Three guesses, then you pay a penalty."

She pursed her lips. The box was blue. It was small and square. It came from Tiffany's...

"A bread board?" she asked innocently.

David's lips twitched. "Try again."

"Um...a vacuum cleaner?"

"Last shot, coming up."

"Let's see...a new washing machine?"

He sighed. "Not again."

"Well, that's what happens when you have twins. The washing machine just works itself to death."

"Yeah." He smiled. "And you've used up all three guesses, Mrs. Adams. So I guess you'll just have to pay the penalty."

Joanna laughed softly. "Oh, my."

His grin turned wickedly sexy. "Oh, my, indeed."

"At least let me see what's in that box..."

"Uh-uh," he said, taking it out of her reach. "Not until you pay up."

Joanna batted her snow-tipped lashes at him. "Why, Mr. Adams, sir, whatever do you have in mind?"

David put his lips to his wife's ear and whispered exactly what he had in mind. She turned pink, laughed softly, and buried her face in his neck.

"That sounds wonderful. When?"

"Tonight, right after the kids are in bed. I'll build a fire, we'll open some champagne..."

Joanna's smile faded. She leaned back in her husband's arms and looked into his eyes. "I love you," she said softly.

David brushed his lips over hers. "My Gypsy," he whispered.

Then, together with their son and daughter, Joanna and David Adams went inside their home and closed the door.

EVER HAD ONE OF THOSE DAYS?

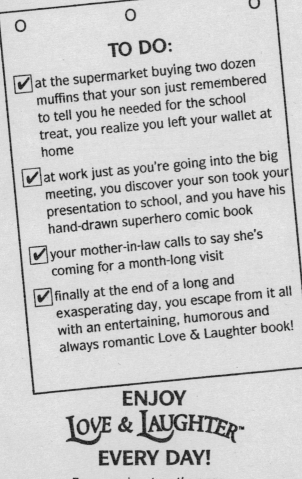

TO DO:

- [x] at the supermarket buying two dozen muffins that your son just remembered to tell you he needed for the school treat, you realize you left your wallet at home

- [x] at work just as you're going into the big meeting, you discover your son took your presentation to school, and you have his hand-drawn superhero comic book

- [x] your mother-in-law calls to say she's coming for a month-long visit

- [x] finally at the end of a long and exasperating day, you escape from it all with an entertaining, humorous and always romantic Love & Laughter book!

ENJOY
LOVE & LAUGHTER™
EVERY DAY!

For a preview, turn the page....

Here's a sneak peek at
Carrie Alexander's THE AMOROUS HEIRESS
Available September 1997...

———————

"YOU'RE A VERY popular lady," Jed Kelley observed as Augustina closed the door on her suitors.

She waved a hand. "Just two of a dozen." Technically true since her grandmother had put her on the open market. "You're not afraid of a little competition, are you?"

"Competition?" He looked puzzled. "I thought the position was mine."

Augustina shook her head, smiling coyly. "You didn't think Grandmother was the final arbiter of the decision, did you? I say a trial period is in order." No matter that Jed Kelley had miraculously passed Grandmother's muster, Augustina felt the need for a little propriety. But, on the other hand, she could be married before the summer was out and be free as a bird, with the added bonus of a husband it wouldn't be all that difficult to learn to love.

She got up the courage to reach for his hand, and then just like that, she—Miss Gussy Gutless Fairchild—was holding Jed Kelley's hand. He looked down at their linked hands. "Of course, you don't really know what sort of work I can do, do you?"

A funny way to put it, she thought absently, cradling his callused hand between both of her own. "We can get to know each other, and then, if that works out..." she murmured. *Wow.* If she'd known what this arranged marriage thing was all about, she'd have been a supporter of Grandmother's campaign from the start!

"Are you a palm reader?" Jed asked gruffly. His voice was as raspy as sandpaper and it was rubbing her all the right ways, but the question flustered her. She dropped his hand.

"I'm sorry."

"No problem," he said, "as long as I'm hired."

"Hired!" she scoffed. "What a way of putting it!"

Jed folded his arms across his chest. "So we're back to the trial period."

"Yes." Augustina frowned and her gaze dropped to his work boots. Okay, so he wasn't as well off as the majority of her suitors, but really, did he think she was going to *pay* him to marry her?

"Fine, then." He flipped her a wave and, speechless, she watched him leave. She was trembling all over like a malaria victim in a snowstorm, shot with hot charges and cold shivers until her brain was numb. This couldn't be true. Fantasy men didn't happen to nice girls like her.

"Augustina?"

Her grandmother's voice intruded on Gussy's privacy. "Ahh. There you are. I see you met the new gardener?"

Let's Celebrate!

LOVE & LAUGHTER™

invites you to the party of the season!

Grab your popcorn and be prepared to laugh as we celebrate with **LOVE & LAUGHTER**.

Harlequin's newest series is going Hollywood!

Let us make you laugh with three months of terrific books, authors and romance, plus a chance to win a FREE 15-copy video collection of the best romantic comedies ever made.

For more details look in the back pages of any Love & Laughter title, from July to September, at your favorite retail outlet.

Don't forget the popcorn!

Available wherever
Harlequin books are sold.

 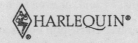 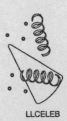

HARLEQUIN®

HARLEQUIN PRESENTS®

More heartwarming romances that feature fantastic men
who *eventually* make fabulous fathers. Ready or not...

August 1997—
YESTERDAY'S BRIDE (#1903)
by Alison Kelly

September 1997—
ACCIDENTAL MISTRESS (#1909)
by Cathy Williams

October 1997—
THE PRICE OF A WIFE (#1914)
by Helen Brooks

FROM HERE TO PATERNITY—
men who find their way to fatherhood
by fair means, by foul, or even by default!

Available wherever Harlequin books are sold.

Don't miss these Harlequin favorites by some of our most popular authors! And now you can receive a discount by ordering two or more titles!

HT#25700	HOLDING OUT FOR A HERO	
	by Vicki Lewis Thompson	$3.50 U.S. ☐/$3.99 CAN.☐
HT#25699	WICKED WAYS	
	by Kate Hoffmann	$3.50 U.S. ☐/$3.99 CAN.☐
HP#11845	RELATIVE SINS	
	by Anne Mather	$3.50 U.S. ☐/$3.99 CAN.☐
HP#11849	A KISS TO REMEMBER	
	by Miranda Lee	$3.50 U.S. ☐/$3.99 CAN.☐
HR#03359	FAITH, HOPE AND MARRIAGE	
	by Emma Goldrick	$2.99 U.S. ☐/$3.50 CAN.☐
HR#03433	TEMPORARY HUSBAND	
	by Day Leclaire	$3.25 U.S. ☐/$3.75 CAN.☐
HS#70679	QUEEN OF THE DIXIE DRIVE-IN	
	by Peg Sutherland	$3.99 U.S. ☐/$4.50 CAN.☐
HS#70712	SUGAR BABY	
	by Karen Young	$3.99 U.S. ☐/$4.50 CAN.☐
HI#22319	BREATHLESS	
	by Carly Bishop	$3.50 U.S. ☐/$3.99 CAN.☐
HI#22335	BEAUTY VS. THE BEAST	
	by M.J. Rodgers	$3.50 U.S. ☐/$3.99 CAN.☐
AR#16577	BRIDE OF THE BADLANDS	
	by Jule McBride	$3.50 U.S. ☐/$3.99 CAN.☐
AR#16656	RED-HOT RANCHMAN	
	by Victoria Pade	$3.75 U.S. ☐/$4.25 CAN.☐
HH#28868	THE SAXON	
	by Margaret Moore	$4.50 U.S. ☐/$4.99 CAN.☐
HH#28893	UNICORN VENGEANCE	
	by Claire Delacroix	$4.50 U.S. ☐/$4.99 CAN.☐

(limited quantities available on certain titles)

	TOTAL AMOUNT	$ _____
DEDUCT:	**10% DISCOUNT FOR 2+ BOOKS**	$ _____
	POSTAGE & HANDLING	$ _____
	($1.00 for one book, 50¢ for each additional)	
	APPLICABLE TAXES*	$ _____
	TOTAL PAYABLE	$ _____
	(check or money order—please do not send cash)	

To order, complete this form, along with a check or money order for the total above, payable to Harlequin Books, to: **In the U.S.:** 3010 Walden Avenue, P.O. Box 9047, Buffalo, NY 14269-9047; **In Canada:** P.O. Box 613, Fort Erie, Ontario, L2A 5X3.

Name: _____

Address: _____ City: _____

State/Prov.: _____ Zip/Postal Code: _____

*New York residents remit applicable sales taxes.
Canadian residents remit applicable GST and provincial taxes.

Look us up on-line at: http://www.romance.net

HBKJS97

Reach new heights of passion and
adventure this August in

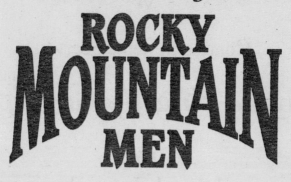

ROCKY MOUNTAIN MEN

Don't miss this exciting new collection featuring
three stories of Rocky Mountain men and the
women who dared to tame them.

CODE OF SILENCE
by Linda Randall Wisdom

SILVER LADY
by Lynn Erickson

TOUCH THE SKY
by Debbi Bedford

Available this August wherever
Harlequin and Silhouette books are sold.

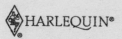 HARLEQUIN®   Silhouette®